SIGNAL 63: REVIVING LONDON

A BROKEN HERO PROTECTOR ROMANCE

THE SIGNAL SERIES
BOOK 2

LC TAYLOR

Cover designed by Rebeca Covers
Edited by Alice I Lunsford
Cover Model Phillip Kitchens

LC Taylor
www.AuthorLCTaylor.com

Behind the Badge Press
www.BehindtheBadgePress.com

He showed me his scars, and in return, he let me pretend that I had none.

—MADELINE MILLER, CIRCE

1

London Brett loved her job—most of the time. But on days like today, she had to remind herself why.

It wasn't easy being a cop… especially as a female. That added more challenges to the job. Hell, every day she had to prove to someone she was strong enough to wear the badge pinned to her chest. At five foot four, most of her fellow officers towered over her, and truth be told, most criminals too. That didn't stop her from showing up and kicking ass every day. She'd been with the Clinton Police Department for ten years. After four years of college, and earning her bachelor's degree in criminal justice, she knew what she wanted to do—be a police officer.

"Well, London? What do you think?" Her partner laughed, pointing towards the drunk now passed out in his own vomit. They'd gotten a call from the bakery downtown about a man who was believed to be dead. Turns out, he was just passed out and covered in his own bodily fluids.

"I think we need to call EMS out to check him." She turned towards the owner. "Ma'am, it'll be a few minutes before he's moved. We are going to have EMS come out and get him, just in case he's hurt."

The owner nodded and went back inside, leaving London and her partner to wait for the fire department. Her partner, Frank, had been with Clinton PD for nearly three decades. He was counting down his days to retirement—so he claimed. London secretly thought he'd work until he died. Frank was propped on the hood of their patrol car, watching her deal with the mess of a man.

"You going to help or just watch?"

"Fuck, leave him there for the medics to deal with."

"Fine." Turning, London saw the ambulance pull up in front of their car. She immediately recognized Alex Boatman, a girl she'd got to know pretty well over the years.

"Hey, Alex. Thanks for responding." She greeted her with a handshake. She'd worked plenty of calls with Alex, not to mention had a few drinks off duty with her. She was surprised to see she had a new partner. "Where's Paul?"

"That old fart? He finally retired. Officer Brett, I'd like you to meet Davey, the newest member of the Clinton Fire Department. He transferred from Wellington."

"Hi, Davey. Nice to meet you. Your patient is this way."

London led the two of them towards the entrance, where the guy was still passed out. London stepped back, appraising the new medic. He looked to be in his late twenties, at least six feet or more, and built like a brick house. He turned, catching her ogling him, and smiled.

"Officer Brett, we got this if you need to head out." His smile was breath-taking, making her feel tingly suddenly.

Uncomfortable with her body's reaction to the new paramedic, she stepped back. "Um… Yeah—you two let me know if there is any new info or you need me. It was nice to meet you, Davey. I'm sure we'll see each other around."

London hurried toward the car, slapping the hood, "Come on, Frank, let's go." She stared out her window, watching the Davey as he and Alex loaded up the patient.

"Alright, alright… geez." He grumbled as he slid into the passenger seat, "What has your panties in a jumble?" Frank turned to look at her, his head swiveling in the direction she was looking. "Oh… I see." He chuckled.

"What do you see?" London spun her head toward him and snapped.

Frank glanced out the window again. "The new paramedic has your attention."

"No, he doesn't." London cranked the engine.

He rumbled with laughter. "I saw you staring just now."

"I was looking at the drunk, you moron." London growled, her eyes rolling at his remark. "I wanted to make sure he wasn't giving them any trouble before we pulled out."

"Right… I'm sure that's what you were doing."

"Fuck off, Frank." London threw the car in reverse. "You hungry?"

Frank grinned. "Do pigs like the mud?"

Raking her eyes over her partner, "Dunno, are you muddy?" She laughed, pointing their car toward the local diner.

"You know, London, it would be alright if you were checking the new guy out. It wouldn't hurt for you to date, you know."

"Awe, Frank… you know I can't date. Men think what I do is intimidating. And I ain't quitting for a cock. So… my vibrator will have to do. But thanks for your concern."

"Jesus Christ, woman. I didn't need to hear about your date with a vibrator. I'm going to have to go home and scrub my brain with bleach to rid that visual. Fuck." he grunted, pushing open his door as he stepped out.

London stuck her tongue out at him. "Well, you started it."

He shook his head as they walked into the Charlie's Diner. "I just said you should date."

"Date… vibrator… what's the difference?"

London laughed as they went inside to eat. She knew Frank meant well, but it was a headache to date. As soon as the guy found out what she did, he'd belittle her. Too many times she sat across from a man, only to have him tell her she was too small to be a cop and how she needed a man to take care of her.

Fuck that.

She didn't need anyone to *take* care of her. London did just fine on her own. If her vibrator wasn't cutting it, she'd go to the bar and find herself a one-night stand. London didn't have any problems getting a dick with no strings attached. She liked it that way, and so did some guys. It was a win-win for everybody.

A boyfriend or husband wasn't something she needed.

Ever.

2

He smelled like vomit. The asshole drunk had woken up just as he was lifting him onto the gurney. Alex had his feet, leaving Davey to raise him under the arms. The idiot opened his eyes, rolled to the side, spewing vomit everywhere—including onto Davey's leg and shoes.

Alex laughed as they climbed back into the rig after dropping the patient off at the ER. "You reek."

"No, shit. That's what vomit will do to you. I'll shower when we get back to the station. I have a spare change of clothes in my locker."

Alex pinched her nose in a dramatic fashion. "Roll down the window, at least."

"Bite me, Alex." Davey laughed as he pressed the button to let the glass down and let fresh air inside the cab. "Hey, who was the officer on the scene?"

"Oh—Officer Brett. She's cool people."

Davey cut his eyes toward her. "You known her long?"

"Why, Davey… do you have a crush?" Alex poked him in the side, grinning like a child.

Shrugging her off, "What? No… I just wondered who she was."

"Well, she's single… and pretty awesome to hang out with."

He kept his eyes on the road as he spoke. "Y'all friends?"

"You could say that… Why you want me to hook you up?"

He chuckled, blowing her suggestion off immediately. "No… I don't date. Just curious is all. London's pretty tiny to be a cop."

"Fuck… don't let her hear you say that she'll kick your ass. She may be small, but I've seen her beat the ever-loving shit outta men twice her size."

Davey visualised the tiny goddess kicking someone's ass. He couldn't help but smile. "I'd pay to see that."

"Someone has a crush." Alex's singsong taunt filled the ambulance.

"Shut up, Alex." Davey elbowed his partner in the ribs.

She tilted her head at him. "Admit it… you think London is hot."

"Fine… she's… cute. But I don't have a crush. I told you. I don't do relationships."

"Why the hell not? You're sexy as shit. You could have any woman you wanted."

"You offering, buttercup?" Davey smirked, knowing damn well Alex preferred ladies.

"What? No… you're like family now—I don't mix work and sex… ever. Plus—you have a cock. But you and London? Yeah, I could totally see you two together."

Davey closed his eyes, trying to push the memory he'd buried years ago. He didn't want to think about it, ever. But meeting Officer Brett stirred something inside of him, something he thought he would never feel again.

As they pulled into the station, Davey sighed in relief. "I'm going to shower and change."

"Ok—meet me in the kitchen when you're done. We aren't finished talking, Davey."

"Great." Davey rolled his eyes. He knew Alex wondered about his past and what had brought him here. He'd tried to avoid talking about it, but with her being his partner, he knew she'd never let up until he gave in and told her.

As soon as Davey stepped into the kitchen, Alex pounced. "Alright, Davey, what's your story? We've been partners long enough now. Tell me, why won't you date?"

He moved to the counter and grumbled. "Damn woman, can't a man get some food first?"

"Nope. Brett is a fine woman, and I think you liked what you saw. Just trying to understand why you wouldn't want to date her. Is it because she's a cop?"

"Fuck no. I just don't do relationships. Too messy." Davey shoved a piece of bread in his mouth.

"Bullshit." Alex glared at him for a second longer. "Whatever, keep your damn secrets."

Davey closed his eyes. "Look, I was engaged. She died."

Alex froze, "Shit. Sorry. I didn't know."

"It's fine. It was a while ago, but I don't want to deal with the mess of a relationship or the feelings that come with it. So lay off me, ok?"

"Yeah…" Alex gave him a caring smile, then turned and walked out, leaving him to stew over his memories. He hated that he just spewed his messy life like that, but he needed her to back off.

Sure, he found officer Brett sexy as hell, but a relationship— nah… not for him. Davey headed into the living room and plopped onto the couch. Just as he propped his feet on the coffee table, the alert for medic blared across the loudspeaker.

So much for resting.

3

"SIR, PLEASE PUT DOWN THE KNIFE." LONDON GRIPPED HER GUN holstered at her side. The last thing she wanted to do was shoot a man, but this man… no—kid, was high on something, and not making any sense. They'd gotten the call about a man acting suspiciously outside a local bar. When she and Frank arrived, the kid was pacing back and forth, waving a knife around.

"NO! Fuck off!" He screamed, pointing at her with the sharp tip.

London watched her partner step closer towards him, "Son… I don't know what's happening right now, but we are here to help you. Can you let us do that? Can you let us help you?"

London heard the ambulance coming to a stop behind her. She didn't glance to check, but she recognised the sound of the bus's air brakes hissing as it parked. She watched as the young man glanced at Frank, confusion written all over his face.

"Drop the knife… that's right." Frank kept encouraging him as she took small steps slowly towards him.

Frank cut his eyes towards her, silently telling her to stop, but London knew this was a make-or-break situation. She watched as the young man gripped his head. The knife pressing against his temple.

"Please… just leave me alone." He squeezed his eyes shut, giving her just the opportunity she'd been waiting for.

London dived at his body, taking him to the ground. She rolled their bodies, placing the young man beneath her. Pushing herself up to her knees, she pinned his hands to the pavement. The knife mashed between his palm and asphalt. Twisting his thumbs, she forced his hands to his back, clicking the cuffs securely in place.

"It's going to be alright…" London looked up to see a wide-eyed Frank, and a very stunned sext paramedic looking on.

"Holy fuck." The paramedic that had been taking up too much residence in her dreams blurted out.

"Damn you, Brett." Frank walked over, helping her off the ground. "You nearly made me shit my pants."

London patted his back as he ushered the man toward the car. "Awe, don't blame your old age and incontinence on me."

Flipping her the bird, Frank groaned. "Funny… real fucking funny."

She dusted off her uniform pants, noting she'd ripped the knee. Turning towards her car, she couldn't stop herself as she winked at Davey.

"That took some major balls." He shook his head. "You could have gotten hurt."

She held her palms up. "Well. I didn't. It all worked out fine."

Davey wore a pinched expression as his head shook. "You shouldn't take chances like that… he was a big guy and had a weapon."

London gritted her teeth. She was used to this response from men—they all thought she should leave the hard police work for the boys. But hearing him say it made her blood spark with anger.

"So, because he's a big guy, I should have stayed away or shot him? Look… Davey, was it?" London stepped forward and poked him in the chest. "Just because I am a *woman*. One who just happens to be petite doesn't mean I can't do this job. In fact, I am pretty sure I could have you on your back before you realised what was happening."

Davey threw his hands up and stepped back. "Fuck. Didn't mean to offend you. And being a woman had nothing to do with my concern… I'd of said the same thing to your partner had he done that."

"Frank?" London laughed. "He'd have a heart attack first… Or shit his pants for real. He can't even get in the car without being winded."

"Now, who's being judgemental?" Davey cocked an eyebrow.

"Whatever." She shrugged. "See ya around, Davey."

Davey watched as she walked off. His blood was pumping hard from how much she got under his skin. He hated how she affected him.

"Hey, Officer Brett?" Davey called out to her as she tugged open the door to get in her patrol car. "I'd like to see you get me on my back in less than five seconds."

"Right. I bet you would." She shot him a cocky smirk as she slipped into the car and closed the door.

Davey grimaced at how it must have come across, slapping his head. "*Shit.*"

"Nice move, moron." Alex patted his back. "It sounded like you just propositioned Officer Brett."

"It's not what I meant. *Fuck.*" Davey Jogged towards the back of the ambulance. "Let's get this guy to the hospital."

"Sure… now you want to work. You get to ride in back. I'm driving."

He'd been standing around staring at Officer Brett while his partner had loaded the patient on her own. "Yeah… fine. Let's go."

Davey climbed into the back of the rig with the guy, who was now passed out and cuffed to the stretcher. His mind wandered back to the moment he watched London tackle him to the ground. It happened so quick, neither he nor Frank had time to intervene. When they finally snapped out of their shocked haze, London already had him cuffed.

And then he went and put his foot in his mouth—unintentionally. Davey was only concerned about her safety, not that she couldn't handle herself. Instead of it coming across that way, she felt like he was attacking her ability to be a good cop. He usually wouldn't give a crap that he'd offended her, but something inside of him clenched with regret. A feeling that he didn't know what to make of sat heavy on his chest.

"You two sleeping back here?" Alex mouthed off as she pulled the door open and peered at Davey.

"Nope… just him. Let's get him inside." Davey helped her pull the gurney out and pushed it inside. He peered around the ER looking for Officer Brett and her partner.

"Don't worry. You're safe. Officer Brett isn't here to put you on your back." Alex laughed, "Let's go. I'm hungry again."

He fully expected her to be there to collect her handcuffs. He wasn't quite ready to face her again. Signing off on the last of the paperwork, Davey met Alex at the rig. He was ready for this shift to end.

4

London sat at the bar listening to her sister carry on about the latest guy in her life. She loved Carrie, but she went through men like underwear. London couldn't stop thinking about the paramedic, Davey. He'd pissed her off so badly, but another side of her couldn't help but be attracted to him.

And that made her even angrier.

Carrie pouted, snapping London from her thoughts. "Are you even listening to me?"

"Um, yeah…" London took a sip of her beer.

"Right. What did I say then?"

London grimaced. "You were, ah, talking about… what's his name?"

"Brad. His name is Brad. What's got you all twisted up, London?" Carrie tilted her head to study London.

"Just thinking about a call from shift. We had a kid waving a knife around, and I tackled him to the ground. One of the paramedics on scene told me I should have been more careful, and it rubbed me wrong."

"Well… He was probably right. You're always acting before thinking."

London gasped, "What? That's not true."

"Yes, it is. You think you have something to prove, so you're always doing stupid shit to look more—I dunno." Carrie threw her hands up in the air. "Macho."

"I do what I need to, to keep everyone safe. I told him I could have him on his back in five seconds, despite his size."

Carrie choked on her drink. "No, you didn't. Is he hot at least?"

"Carrie. I didn't mean it like that. The point was, despite my tiny size, I could easily take him down."

"Right. I'm sure he took it that way. What'd he say?"

London blushed when she remembered his words and the look he had when he realised how they came across. "That he couldn't wait to see me get him on his back in five seconds."

"HOLY SHIT!"

London laughed.

"Exactly."

Carrie waggled her eyebrows. "You're totally going to hook up, right?"

"No." London rolled her eyes.

"Why not?"

Sighing, she tipped her drink to her lips. "I don't date."

"Who said anything about dating? And why don't you date again?"

London took another drink of her beer. "Carrie. We've been over this. Guys are all hot about my job at first… then they go all alpha male on me and demand I get a desk job."

Her sister flipped her hair as she rolled her eyes. "What's wrong with a desk job? Don't you want kids one day? You aren't getting any younger."

"Fuck you, sis. And I don't think that's in the plans for me. Unless I find a man, who can handle all of me… my job included. Marriage and babies are not going to happen."

Carrie's head shook with disappointment. "That's sad. Mom would want you to marry someone and be happy."

"That's not fair. Don't bring mom into this." London shot her sister a threatening glare.

"Fine. Whatever. But back to what I said. Who needs to date… whatever his name is, to have sex?"

"His name is Davey, and I don't think he's into me like that, Carrie."

"But are *you* into him like that?"

"I mean… he's hot. Who wouldn't be?" London giggled, swallowing more of the amber liquid. "But I have no intention of asking him to hook up."

Alex slid onto the stool next to London. "Asking who to hook up?"

"A hot new paramedic she worked a call with." Carrie smiled.

"*CARRIE.*" London dropped her head into her hands.

Alex's face bust into a massive grin. "Wait… Davey? Fuck, this is good. He's totally into you."

"Told you." Carrie folded her arms across her chest. "I told London she should totally hook up with him. But miss," She made air quotes with her fingers, "I don't date anyone—said no."

"I think you should go for it. He needs to get laid. Think of it as donating to charity. Do it for your fellow female public safety workers…" Alex tapped the bar.

"You two are ridiculous. I'm not going to fuck your partner. And no one that looks *like* that is a charity case. Jesus."

"Hello, ladies."

London nearly swallowed her tongue at the timber voice. There, standing behind her, was Davey. She closed her eyes, praying he hadn't heard her last comment. She wanted to stab her sister and Alex with a plastic fork right now.

Alex smirked, turning to her partner. "Hey, Davey. You remember London Brett. And this is her sister Carrie."

"Nice to meet you, Carrie. London." Davey tilted his head towards her. "I just popped in with the guys from the station and thought I'd say hello. I'll leave you to it. I don't want to interrupt."

Alex nodded towards her other teammates. "I'll catch up with y'all later."

"Sure. And London," Davey paused before walking off. "I am all about *donating* to charity. Let me know if you have any good ones in mind."

London choked on her beer, spewing it all over her sister, and Alex. Alex and Carrie were doubled over in a fit of giggles. Clearly, he'd heard what she'd said. London was mortified as she glanced over at her supposed friend and sister. "Shut the fuck up, you two."

5

Davey sat at the table with his fellow firemen. They'd accepted him as one of their own when he joined.

"Brett hasn't stopped eye-fucking you, Davey. Maybe you should go back over there and put her out of her misery." Jason Hunter, the captain on the engine, laughed as he popped a peanut in his mouth.

Davey grinned, peering over his shoulder. He was pleased to see Alex and London were gawking at him from the place at the bar. Tilting his beer at the two women in salute, he chuckled as they turned their backs on him.

"She's a feisty one." Davey set his nearly empty bottle down. "But I seriously don't think she's interested in a hook-up."

"You're kidding, right?" Jonesy gave him a pointed glare. "All she does is hook up. She doesn't do relationships either. But she is pretty picky—you probably aren't good enough for her."

Davey looked over at London again. The girls had paid their tab and were making their way towards the door. Davey tossed a few bills on the table and stood. "Catch you later, guys."

"I don't blame you, Davey. She's fucking hot." Uri smiled. "See you on shift, brother." Davey high-fived the two men and followed the ladies out.

"London," he jogged to catch up to her and Alex, "Hang on a second."

"Hey, Davey." Alex smiled at him, "Um, London, I'll see you around."

She leaned against her car, glaring at the sexy paramedic as her friend walked away. Sure, see you later. What do you want, Davey?" London folded her arms across her chest and looked him over. There was no denying how good he looked.

"Um… I guess I'll catch you later, sis." London realized her sister Carrie was watching their interaction.

She caught her smiling at them and rolled her eyes. "I'll call you tomorrow, sis."

Carrie tossed a wave and hurried off towards her car.

"Alright, be careful on shift. See you around, Davey, it was nice meeting you."

"See you later." He tossed a subtle wave in her direction before turning back to face London. "I just…" Davey swallowed. "Would you like to grab dinner with me sometime?"

London's brows knitted together. "Dinner? Like a date?"

"We don't have to call it a date if it makes you uncomfortable. How about dinner between new friends?"

London shifted nervously on her feet. She couldn't stop staring at the man in front of her. Part of her wanted to jump in her car and hightail it for the hills, but a small piece of her wanted to give in and throw caution to the wind.

She pulled her door open and got in her car. "Fine. Dinner as friends."

"Wait," Davey reached out and grabbed her arm. "Give me your number so I can call you."

London pulled her phone out and unlocked the screen. "Here, put it in my phone."

Davey typed his number into her contacts and then sent himself a text. "There, now I can text you. I'll be calling you soon, in London."

"Night, Davey." London snatched her phone and slipped into her car.

Closing her eyes, she sighed. What the hell was she doing? Davey was hot, and her lady parts wanted her to follow him out of the parking lot and have her way with him. Instead, she started her car and pulled off. She had an early shift and needed to get home. London had given him her number, but that didn't mean she had to follow through with a date.

Davey watched as London drove off. His heart was beating a mile a minute. He hadn't had this reaction to a woman since Carley. Just thinking about her made the guilt creep in. Carley was the woman he'd planned forever with—only to have her and their dreams of forever ripped from his life.

Davey sat behind the steering wheel of his truck. Glancing at the clock, he groaned when he discovered it was nearly midnight. He had to be on shift at 8 am. Cranking the engine, he glanced at the empty spot London's car had been parked and shook his head. He just needed to get laid—that was all this was.

Right?

Davey refused to let his heart get attached to anyone again. There was no way he would ever let himself feel the profound loss he'd felt when Carley died.

He'd been ripped to shreds the day he'd got the call she was gone. She had just left the church, ensuring the flowers had arrived safely and were ready for their wedding in three days. She was supposed to be meeting him for dinner, so Davey waited at the restaurant. He'd tried calling her phone only to get her voice mail when she didn't show on time. It wasn't until his sister Harley called, urging him to get to the hospital—that he realized why Carley hadn't shown up.

She'd been hit by a dump truck running a red light. When the truck t-boned her car, Carley'd been crushed by the steering wheel. By the time he got to the hospital, she was gone. Davey stood in the emergency room, listening to the doctor drone on. Her mother sobbed as Carley's father held her. Harley's tears flooded down her cheeks as she tried to console him. But Davey could only stand there—the engagement ring the nurse handed him was wrapped tightly in his fist, tucked in his pocket. The doctor offered to let Davey say goodbye, but he couldn't. He didn't want to remember her like that. Davey shoved her engagement ring into his sister's hand and walked out of the hospital. The next few days, he found himself in a fog. Her funeral had been beautiful, held on the day they were to be married.

He tried to find his place in life. Becoming a paramedic had been his way of healing. For the first couple of years, he worked in their hometown, but Wellington held too many painful memories. When the position opened in the neighboring town, he put in for a transfer. He was relieved when he got it. Packing all his belongings, he bid farewell to his family and moved to Clinton.

Pulling into his driveway, Davey shook the bitter memories from his head. A couple hours of sleep would do him good, then work would help fill the emptiness he felt inside.

6

London breezed through the locker room and grabbed her things. Frank was waiting outside for her, leaning against the patrol car.

"Glad to see you… I'm starving."

London laughed, "You're always hungry, Frank. Let's go. We can grab a bite before the shit hits the fan."

Frank slid into the passenger seat and slammed his door. "What's crawled up your butt this morning, London?"

London cocked her eyebrow at him. "What the fuck you talking about?"

"You're moody. You need to get laid or something."

"Why you worrying about my vagina, Frank?"

Frank scoffed, "Jesus Christ, woman… I ain't worrying about your," he waved his hand toward her, "stuff… I simply said you needed to get laid. How about that paramedic?"

"Drop it, Frank." London pulled the car into the Waffle House and hopped out. She didn't want to talk about Davey—or her vagina.

They'd barely gotten their food swallowed when their radios went off. Another domestic.

"Great…" London stood and tossed a few bills on the table. "Let's go, Frank. Someone's happy marriage needs our counseling services."

"God damn idiots." Frank pushed himself out of the booth and grumbled all the way to the car. The call wound up being a joke. The husband and wife were arguing over what color to paint their bedroom. The wife threw the paintbrush at the husband, who in turn threw the entire paint bucket at her. She'd called 911 out of anger, but once they'd gotten on the scene, she was sobbing and apologizing for overreacting. Frank and London made sure they were good and left them at home to work it out. Neither was a threat. They were just tense and exploded over something stupid.

Frank and London parked the car in an empty lot, catching up on paperwork. The day had passed slowly, with a few simple calls here and there, but nothing worth a bucket of salt.

"London," Frank broke the silence, "Don't you think you deserve to be happy?"

"What makes you think I'm not happy?"

"You avoid relationships like they're the plague. Why is that?"

"You know why, Frank. Men can't handle me being a police officer. It's emasculating to them. And I don't plan on quitting my job for a man. Ever."

"But what about a family? Don't you want one?"

"I don't know. Maybe. But it would take a strong man to handle me and my career. That's why I keep things loose."

"Are we talking about your vagina again?"

London hit him, "Asshole."

The sound of the radio broke their reverie. A car accident with injuries a few blocks from where they were meant it was time to work. Flicking on the lights and siren, London pulled onto the roadway. Her gut churned, wondering if Davey would be the responding paramedic.

When they got on the scene, London sucked in a breath. A small sedan had been struck by an SUV in the intersection. Throwing the car in park, she jumped out of her seat and rushed towards the car. The driver of the sedan, a young woman, was crushed beneath the dashboard. A toddler was crying in the back seat, his car seat still buckled in, securing him completely.

"Hey, little man, I'm going to help you, ok?" London tried to pull the door open but found it jammed. "Frank!" She hollered for her partner.

"London, EMS is pulling up now." Frank rushed to her side. "Fuck…" He looked inside at the woman, "Is she…"

"I don't know." London cut him off. "Help me get to him."

Frank rounded the car, pulling the back-passenger door open and slid into the seat beside the boy. "Hey there, fella. Let me look at you." Frank checked him over. "He looks ok, but I'm going to pull his whole seat out, keep him in it."

"Ok." London turned her attention to the woman. "Ma'am… Can you hear me?" She tried to feel for a pulse, but she was covered in blood. London turned to see Davey running towards her.

"*Move.*" He shouted at her, shoving her out of the way. Davey quickly assessed the driver and shouted out for the jaws of life. He looked frantic, almost possessed, as he tried to help the victim. London stepped back, realizing the other driver was seated on the curb, looking as though he'd just run a marathon, not rammed his SUV into another car. Walking toward him, "Sir, are you hurt?"

"No… Christ, she didn't stop. She just blew through the red light. I tried to stop… but… oh my God—did I kill her?"

London squatted down beside him, "Let's get you checked out, ok?" She helped him stand and walked him to another ambulance that had arrived on scene. She stood by as the EMT checked on him. Once he'd been given the ok, London spoke. "Is there someone I can call for you?"

"Is she dead?" The man's eyes followed the woman who'd finally been pulled free from the car. She was being rushed towards the back of the ambulance, Davey running alongside her.

"I don't know."

London watched as the young man burst into tears. She knew this was hard to get over, even if it wasn't his fault. The witnesses had all confirmed that the woman had been the one to run the red light. London patted his back. "Come on, let me give you a ride somewhere."

"It's alright, I called my wife. She's on her way." As soon as he spoke, a woman rushed towards him. She pulled him into her arms as he sobbed against her. The young woman nodded at London.

"Thank you." She smiled, taking London's card as she guided her husband toward her awaiting car.

London found Frank and ushered him towards the patrol car. This had been one hell of a way to end the shift, but she was glad to be heading back to the station. She couldn't shake the terror she'd seen in Davey's eyes as he helped the driver of the other car. It was something more profound than just witnessing a victim in a car.

7

"WHAT'VE YOU GOT PLANNED FOR THE NIGHT, LONDON?" FRANK asked as they walked out of the building. London had changed out of her uniform, now donning a pair of skinny jeans and a loose-fitting t-shirt. Even though she had her jacket on, she couldn't avoid shuddering from the cold air.

"Damn, it's getting cold." She blew her hot breath into her hands.

"Avoiding the question, I see." Frank chuckled.

"Nah—just trying to get warm. Actually, I might swing by the fire station. That call really seemed to shake the newbie up."

Frank's eyes grew wide. "Well damn. Didn't see that coming."

"What? I just want to make sure he and Alex are alright."

"Fine… Fine. I'll see you in the morning."

London waved him off as she pulled her door shut. She knew it might send the wrong message, but she was genuinely concerned. His eyes held terror—pure, gut-wrenching fear. She just needed to make sure he was okay. Then she'd go home.

Parking in an empty spot, she pulled her jacket tight as she headed towards the open bay. She spotted Alex immediately.

"Hey, Alex!" London called out to her friend.

"London," Alex smacked a guy on the arm, "Come on in. You remember Jonesy." She tilted her head towards him, smirking.

"Yeah, hey Jonesy. How's it going?"

"Been a rough shift so far. You—just getting off duty?"

"Yep. Y'all heard anything about the car accident victim?"

Alex glanced at her feet, her shoulders dropping. "The woman died. Kid's alright though—just some scratches and bruises."

"Shit." London ran her hands through her hair. "That's awful. Witnesses told two officers on the scene that she had turned around towards her kid. She didn't even attempt to stop." She shook her head, thinking about that kid who lost his mother. London didn't know much about her. She wondered if she'd been married.

"Yeah. Some of the crew aren't taking it well." Alex shrugged.

"Davey?" London asked.

She nodded. "He hasn't come out of his bunk. It really messed with his head. I mean, I get it—his fiancé died in a similar way…"

London sucked in a breath. "He upstairs?"

Alex smiled. "You going up?"

"I just need to see he's ok. His expression on the scene is messing with my head. It was…" London shook her head and paused. "I get it now. But can I go up?"

"Sure. I'll tell the guys to give you some privacy. Maybe you can talk him out of his funk."

"It's not like that, Alex. He's a friend… barely." London started up the stairs and headed down the narrow hallway.

The station was two stories. On the first floor were the kitchen, dining area, and gathering room. Upstairs was divided into six individual rooms. Each holding two beds—enough to house twelve men or women. At the end of the hall was a large bath-room. Alex had told London how she got to use it all alone since she was the only female on shift. Most of the guys treated her like a sister—which drove her nuts most of the time.

Stopping at the only closed door, London knocked. At first, there was no response. Raising her hand to knock again, she jumped as the door was snatched open.

"Alex, I told you to leave me…" Davey paused. "Shit, London. I thought you were Alex again. She doesn't follow directions very well."

"True words. But no. It's me. I wanted to check on you. I heard about the victim." London shoved her hands in her pockets and smiled.

He opened the door and motioned her inside."And you came here… to check on me?"

"Yes… No, I mean. Look, you seemed pretty rattled on the scene. I was worried."

"Worried?" He pushed the door shut. "About me?"

London walked towards the window, looking out into the dark sky. "I guess."

Davey moved to stand behind her. "I'm glad you're here." His hot breath breezed across her neck. London squeezed her eyes closed. She hated how she responded to him.

"Davey," her voice was filled with a warning. "Just friends, remember?" She darted around him. "Maybe this was a mistake." Gripping the doorknob, Davey bolted and pressed his hands against the wood, caging her in.

"Don't tell me you don't feel the chemistry between us."

"I don't…" London swallowed. "Do relationships, Davey. They're messy."

"I don't do them either. I wasn't talking about a relationship, London." He tugged her arm and spun her around. His knee pressed between her legs as he pinned her arms above her head.

"Tell me you don't want this, and I'll stop."

London stared into his eyes. She blinked, trying to tell herself why this was a mistake, but leaned forward and pressed her lips to his. Davey groaned into her mouth as his body pressed into hers. She ground against his knee, arching into him. London had never been kissed like Davey was kissing her. His mouth slipped down, kissing her chin, her jaw, then settling on the curve of her neck.

"God. You're fucking beautiful." He nipped at her flesh, his hands releasing her wrists and slipping beneath her legs. He hoisted her up, pressing her into the door harder. Her legs wrapped around his waist, her center grinding against the steel bulge in his pants.

"Oh, God!" She fisted his hair, their lips colliding, as Davey slipped his hand around her waist, freeing the button to her jeans. His hand slid beneath the zipper and into her panties. London gasped as Davey buried his finger into her channel. He fingered her as he continued to nip and bite at her neck. London couldn't stop the moan that slipped out.

"That's it, baby." Davey pushed in another digit, curving them into the spot that forced London over the edge. Her pussy clamped down on his fingers, spasming and flooding a pool of come down over his knuckles.

"Davey!" She squealed, her orgasm washing over her as he slipped his hand from her pants. London watched as Davey licked his fingers and then pressed a kiss to her lips. He set her down, his hands pressed firmly against the wooden door. It hit London what they'd just done and where they were.

"Fuck." She pushed under his arm.

"What?"

"That shouldn't have happened. We are at your job, for Christ's sake." London paced the room.

Davey propped himself against the door. "It's not like the others haven't brought a girl up to their rooms. Calm down."

"Calm down? Are you serious right now? This," She waved a finger between them, "is not why I came here."

Davey snatched her hand, tugging her into his chest. "I know. But it happened." He lifted her chin with his finger. "And I don't regret it. Do you?"

She closed her eyes, trying to get her heart to stop beating ninety miles an hour. "I don't know."

"Have dinner with me?" Davey asked.

London jerked from him. "I…" the alarm blared, cutting through her words.

She watched as Davey pulled the door open. "I'll pick you up at eight. That should give you enough time to get home and change. See you tomorrow night. And London," London glanced at him, "We will finish this later." He darted down the hall, leaving her to stare at the vacant spot he'd been standing in.

London sighed and ambled out. The station was empty, giving her a chance to sneak out and not face anyone. Huffing out a breath, she got in her car. London had a feeling she was in trouble.

8

Davey pulled into London's driveway at eight. Alex had been gracious enough to give him her address since London had avoided his calls and texts. He knew she was a tough cookie, needing to assert her dominance. Usually, he didn't go for the dominating women, but something about London had him all tied up in knots. And after their heavy make-out session, he wanted more. The taste of her juices was still on his tongue. Her face and the flush of her skin when she came left him with some naughty dreams. Lucky enough, no one at the station said anything to him about her visit.

Alex simply smiled and said that London had finally met her match—but didn't elaborate. London had been pretty clear on not wanting a relationship, and so had Davey, until last night. There was something about her that made him think, just maybe there could be more. Shaking his head, he got out of his truck and went to her door.

"Davey," London pulled open the door, "You actually came."

"I said eight, didn't I?"

"Yeah, come in. I need to finish getting ready." Davey followed her in realizing that she'd answered the door in just a shirt and panties.

"Do you always answer the door dressed like that?" Davey smirked.

"Fuck off. I'll be out in a minute."

Davey had to adjust his cock, which was painfully hard in his pants. He hadn't had a reaction like this to a woman since… Carley. Guilt washed over him.

"You alright?" London's voice snapped him from his thoughts.

"Sure—you hungry?"

"Nah uh… what had you so lost in thought just now? It looked pretty serious."

"Nothing."

"I don't believe you. I won't have dinner with you if you can't be honest. What is it?" She propped her arm on the counter, waiting for him to answer.

Davey stared at London. She was beautiful. Her long brown hair, typically pulled into a tight ponytail, hung loosely on her shoulders. She was dressed in a pair of leggings and a long sweater that hung off one shoulder.

"I… um…" Davey swallowed.

"Is this about your fiancé?" London folded her arms across her chest.

"What?" Davey blinked.

"Alex told me. She said that's why you don't do relationships. If this," She did air quotes. "Dinner as friends is too much. You can leave. You're the one who asked, remember?"

Davey couldn't believe what he heard. Alex had told his business. He wanted to be mad, but he wasn't. He was relieved. "No. well, kind of. I don't do relationships because losing someone you love like that ruins you. But I don't want you to leave—just know I'm emotionally fucked up."

"We're all emotionally constipated, Davey. What you went through was awful. I don't judge you. And I don't do relationships either, remember?"

"Why is that London? You're a beautiful woman. You should have tons of men knocking down your door."

London snorted, "Funny. But no… no doors falling off the hinges. Men can't handle my job. And it's the only thing I've ever wanted in life. So, I stick to casual sex. I won't give up my career for a man—and that usually means the end of a relationship."

"Sounds to me like you've been dating the wrong guys, London."

"Well, when you find one that can handle a dominating, foul mouth woman, who happens to don a badge and a gun, then maybe we'll talk." She laughed.

Davey moved so fast London didn't react. He pulled her into his arms and set her on the edge of the countertop. Davey pressed his lips to hers, his tongue slipping between the seam of her lips. London fisted his hair, giving in to his demands.

After a heated exchange, Davey pulled away and rested his forehead on hers. "What are you doing to me?" He helped her down, pressing another kiss to her swollen lips, "Dinner?"

"Um… sure. Dinner," London grabbed her boots and slipped them on.

"London," Davey smiled, "If we don't go now, I'm afraid we won't leave your place."

London stopped. "Right… well, let's go."

Davey pulled into a local pizza place and cut the engine. "Pizza ok with you?"

"Absolutely. Plus, this place has the best view of the water." London hopped out of his truck and met him at the hood. Living in a coastal town meant having magnificent views and plenty to do in the summer. He walked beside her, resisting the urge to pull her hand in his; instead, he placed his palm at the small of her back.

The hostess led them to a booth towards the back. The waitress appeared and took their order. "So… what made you come to Clinton?"

"Well," Davey took a sip of his water, "When my fiancée died, I tried to move on. Working with the fire department helped fill the hole she left behind… But."

"It wasn't enough?" London smiled.

"No, it wasn't. She was everywhere. I needed to have a fresh start. So, when the position opened here, I took it. It's been a couple of good weeks, though."

"Tell me about her—your fiancée. I mean, if it's not too hard."

Davey was blown away by London. She had this tough exterior, but inside, she was a caring person. "No, it's easier now. Her name was Carley. We met as freshmen in college. It was love at first sight, at least for her." He laughed. "I was a dick to her. But she persisted, and well… the rest is history. She was a firecracker. Carley wanted to be a nurse, and she would have been. After three years, I decided I couldn't see my life without her. I popped the question. We had only one year left of college, but we didn't want to wait—the wedding was going to happen over Christmas break. Everything was planned. I'd just talked to her. She was leaving the church and meeting me for dinner. Carley was always on time. I think I knew deep down something was wrong, but I sat there waiting. My sister Harley called me. I remember the moment the doctor came out and told me she was gone. He handed me her ring. I was so numb. Hell," he took another drink, "Until now, I've just been walking around like a corpse."

London slid her hand across the table. "That had to have been hard. I'm so sorry, Davey."

Davey ran his fingers over her knuckles. "It gets easier every day. Plus," He pulled her hand up and kissed her hand, "new friends are making me remember what it's like to live."

She pulled her hand from his. "Glad I can help." She glanced at her watch. "Shit, is it really that late?"

Davey looked at his phone, realizing they'd been talking for hours. "Damn—I'm sorry. I didn't realize how late it had gotten. I should get you home. You have an early shift."

Davey paid the tab and walked London out. "I had a lot of fun tonight. Think we could do this again?"

"I'd like that, Davey. Text me your schedule so we can work something out…Ok?"

Davey dropped London off at her house, pressing a kiss to her lips. "I'd offer to walk you up, but I think we both know if I do that, you won't be getting any sleep. Text me soon."

London smiled and ran up the steps to her door. Her heart was thumping against her ribs, telling her that this was dangerous territory.

But she liked Davey. A *lot*.

9

London couldn't hide the smile on her face when she slipped into the patrol car next to Frank.

"What's with the creepy grin, London?" Frank pulled his seatbelt over and clicked it into place.

"I can't smile without you saying it's creepy. Jeez… I'm just in a good mood. Is that a crime?"

"Did you get laid or something? I've never seen you so… I don't know. Glowy."

"Glowy? Who the fuck says that? Do you talk to your wife like that, Frank?"

"I say all kinds of things to my wife. It's why we have five kids —cause my dirty talk gets her hot and…"

"EEEEWWW… I do not want to hear about your private shit. Plus, Kathy would kick your ass if she knew you were telling her business."

"Please… Kathy knows I talk. And she likes you. She even said you needed to get laid."

London couldn't help but laugh. Frank was your typical Italian man. He was loud and didn't care what came out of his mouth. He and his wife, Kathy, had been married forever. You couldn't help but be envious. London put the car in gear and hit the street.

The day had gone pretty slow, but just as Frank and London were pulling in to grab a bite to eat, a call came out about a fight at one of the local pubs.

"Christ… it's only one in the afternoon," Frank grumbled.

"Yep—and you know what happens when they drink… someone gets their feelings hurt over something stupid."

London pulled the car into the parking lot and jumped out, "Come on, Frank… let's go get dirty."

"You're one fucked up girl. I can think of much better ways to get dirty." London snorted as they pulled the door open. Immediately, she ducked as a chair flew past the opening and smashed onto the pavement between them. "Well, fuck." Frank stepped inside.

"POLICE!" He yelled, garnering the attention of a few patrons. Several scampered backward, revealing two large guys locked together in the middle of the floor. Several tables were smashed, and the bartender was screaming at them to stop. A couple more officers joined them inside. Frank grabbed one of the men's arms and pulled him backward. "Knock it off, asshole." The other jumped up and charged at them.

London jumped forward, wrapping her arm around his chest. He pushed at her, trying to get at the other man. "Calm down!" She screamed in his ear. The man threw his arm back, catching her off guard, and struck her in the face.

"You *FUCKING* idiot." London saw red, threw her leg out, and swept his foot, taking him to the ground. He landed with a thud but tugged her down with him. His size amassed her as he lunged at her gun. London fought, keeping her hand securely over her holster. She drew her knee up, catching him in the balls. He grunted and released the handle of her gun. London jerked her elbow up, catching him in the nose. As she pushed up, someone was pulling him off her.

"LONDON!" Frank screamed, pulling her off the ground. "FUCKING DIPSHIT!" he kicked at the man now being cuffed by the backup officers. His nose poured blood from where London had clocked him. "Are you ok?" Frank patted her down, checking for injuries.

"FRANK!" London jerked away from him. "I'm fine. Christ." But even as she said it, the adrenaline wore off, and she wavered —dizziness wracking her body. She bent at the knees and vomited.

"Damn it." She screamed. Her head ached, reaching up she felt wetness. Pulling her hand away, she found her fingers covered in blood. "*Shit.*"

"You should get that checked out. It looks like you may need some stitches. Come on," Frank grabbed her arm. "The others got this. I'm taking you to the hospital."

London sat as the emergency room doctor cleaned her cut. "Not too deep, just a butterfly, and you'll be good to go."

"Thanks." She scooped up her things and met Frank outside. "Good as new."

"Right…" Frank shook his head. "That guy could have killed you."

"He didn't."

Frank clicked his tongue. "You are reckless, London."

"So… What was I supposed to do? Just let him attack you. What kind of partner would that make me?"

"Fine. Just be careful next time. Seriously, I need you to take care of yourself—you're the best partner I've ever had… don't go getting yourself killed. I don't want to train someone new."

London smirked. Frank was a big softy inside. She sat in the passenger seat, watching his profile, when her phone vibrated in the console. Frank quirked an eye at her as London snatched it up. She tried to hide the smile, but Frank caught her.

"Who might that be?" He chuckled.

London read the text message. "A friend."

Davey: I have tomorrow off. Feel like coming to dinner tonight when you get off?

London: What time? I'll bring wine.

Davey: Whenever you can get here. I'll be cooking.

London: Great—see you in a few hours.

Davey: :-)

Frank pulled into the station and cut the engine. "You need any help with the paperwork?"

"Nah—I'll get the report typed up before I leave."

"Alright then," Frank pulled open the door, "I'll see you in a couple of days. Holler if you need anything."

London hurried to get the report done. She was eager to get home and change. Davey, cooking her dinner, excited her. She needed to escape the day, and he was just the way to do that.

10

Davey was busy at the stove when he heard the knock at his door. Putting the spoon down, he wiped his hands and opened the door. London held up a bottle of wine. "Glasses?"

Davey stepped to the side and ushered her in. "Damn—bad day at work?"

London turned to him, smiling, but Davey hissed when he saw the black and blue mark on her temple. His finger immediately went to the butterfly strip stuck to her skin. "What the fuck?"

"Just another day at work. Now…" She spun, setting the bottle on the counter, "How bout' a glass?"

Davey shook his head, trying to calm his nerves. Seeing her hurt did something to him, and he didn't want to say something that would piss her off again.

Grabbing two glasses from the cabinet, he opened the bottle and poured the sweet liquid into them, filling them up to the rims. "Seriously, what happened?"

"Bar fight. What is that delicious smell?" She brushed him off, walking towards the stove and stirred the sauce. Putting the spoon to her lips, she blew on it before placing it in her mouth.

"Oh, God." She moaned around the metal utensil, the sound going straight to his cock. "This is fantastic."

"Thanks." Davey willed his body under control and plated food. He set them down on the table and pulled the bread from the oven. "Let's eat."

London didn't speak as she shoved her mouth full. Davey could barely control himself as she made the sexiest noise with each bite. He'd never been so turned on by watching someone eat. "You like it?" He smiled.

London chuckled, "Yeah—sorry. I didn't realize how hungry I was. You can cook for me anytime."

He grinned as he stood, carrying their dishes to the sink. Topping off their glasses with wine, he walked towards the couch. "Want to watch something on T.V.?" He turned to find London biting her lip. She grabbed the glass from his hand and set it down on the coffee table. Pushing him down, she straddled his lap.

"No. I don't want to watch television." She leaned forward and pressed her lips to his.

Davey's hands gripped her hips and ground her down on the hard ridge of his pants. Their tongues danced, her moans driving him crazy. London ran her hands up his arms, slipping them beneath the sleeves of his shirt.

"Fuck." He pulled her shirt up over her head and palmed her tits. "You're beautiful."

He leaned forward and nipped the pink bud beneath the black lace bra she wore. Reaching behind herself, London undid the clasp and freed her breasts. He sucked in a sharp breath before diving forward and sucking her exposed nipple between his lips. She dug her hips into his cock, eliciting a groan from him. He stood, walking her backwards as he navigated her to his room. Their lips never separated, and he somehow got them there without cause. He kicked the door closed as he tossed her to the bed.

Stepping back, he stripped himself of his shirt. London bit her lip and climbed up on her knees, grabbing at the front of his pants. Fumbling with the button, she got it open and slipped her hand into his boxers. Her fingers wrapped around his length, causing him to buck his hips into her. "Fuck." He hissed as she stroked him.

Davey pushed her back, causing her hand to release her hold on him. He ripped her leggings off her body, leaving her completely bare. He pushed her legs apart and dove between her thighs like a wild animal.

London bucked, moaning and writhing beneath him. His tongue flicked across her tiny pearl, sending shock waves up her spine. "Oh. God… please." She panted beneath him. "I need… I need." London begged, unsure of what she needed.

"Let go, baby. I want to hear your screams as I fuck you." He dived back in, lapping her juices and sucking on her clit. London couldn't hold back and let out a howl, arching off the bed.

Davey stood, smiling as he pulled his jeans down. "I'm not done yet."

He rolled a condom on his hard length and climbed over her. His lips found her neck as he lined his dick up with her soft folds. As he pressed his lips to hers, he buried his cock inside her channel. He paused, allowing her to adjust to his size. Davey knew she'd been with other men, but he was built big everywhere. He didn't want to hurt her.

London wiggled beneath him, pulling on his shoulders to urge him to move. Davey needed no more convincing. He thrust in and out, listening to her mewl beneath him. Her pants and whimpers drove him wild with need. His cock had never been so hard —not even with Carley. "That's it. I want to feel you come on my cock, London."

She bucked and moved beneath him. He could feel her cunt squeezing his length. "You like it when I talk dirty? Give me what I want, London. Squeeze me…" He pressed his forehead to hers. "That's it… just like that. I can feel your pussy milking my cock. Do you feel it? How your body responds to mine… I want you to come all over my dick. Do it…" Davey leaned back and thrust his back, pushing his tip deep inside her. London screamed out just as her core locked down on him. He nearly blacked out, his orgasm bursting from him like an explosion. He collapsed, rolling to his side, and tugged her against him.

What they just shared felt like an out-of-body experience. "Holy Shit."

"Holy Shit is right." London giggled, "That was…"

"Amazing." Davey finished for her.

Davey rolled out of bed and disappeared into the bathroom. When he came out, he had a towel in his hand. He wiped the sweat from his chest before cleaning off London. He sat on the edge of the bed and ran his hand up her side. "You're amazing, London." His fingers trailed up her body, coming to rest on the white strip at her temple.

London grabbed his hand. "It's nothing."

Davey's face contorted. "You could have been hurt worse."

"It's part of the job. I'm fine, I promise."

Davey growled, unable to control his need to protect her. "But you could get hurt. I don't like it."

London pushed his hand off and slipped out of bed. "It's my job, Davey. Yeah… I can get hurt, but I knew that when I became a cop." London pulled her leggings on. She stormed out of the room and grabbed her shirt and bra. Slipping them on, she pulled on her shoes.

"Where are you going?" Davey followed her to the door.

"Home. I knew this was a mistake. Every guy is the same. Being a cop is all I know… it's been my dream since I was a kid. Thanks for dinner." London stormed out, leaving Davey to stare at the wooden door. He didn't understand what happened. One minute she had been in his arms, the next, she was storming out like she was on fire. He hadn't meant to imply he didn't like her being a cop. He was merely suggesting he didn't enjoy seeing her hurt.

Davey ran his palm down his face. "Fuck." He cursed into the empty room.

He'd give her some space, then try to reason with her. After thinking he never wanted a relationship again, London burst into his life all lights and sirens. He wasn't going to just walk away—not yet. Locking the door, he crawled into bed, her scent still covering his sheets. Grabbing his phone, he sent her a quick text, telling her he'd give her space, but he wasn't done talking about this. Of course, she didn't respond.

Davey drifted off to sleep, the memory of her skin fresh in his mind.

11

"ARE YOU JUST GOING TO AVOID DAVEY FOR THE REST OF YOUR life?" Alex asked, swallowing the amber liquid she held in her hand.

"I don't know. He's just like all the other men. They want to act like it's OK I'm a cop, but then they try to change me. It's who I am. I won't give it up—regardless of how good of a cock they have."

Carrie snorted. "So, you admit his cock is good?"

They were sitting at the pub, having drinks on her last day off. She just needed to put things in perspective, but her sister and friend weren't helping.

"That's all you heard?"

"Well?" Alex prodded. "Don't keep us in suspense. How was it?"

London sighed, "Fucking amazing."

"I knew it!" Carrie clapped. "You like him."

"Until he got macho about my job."

Alex furrowed her brows. "Wait... that doesn't sound like Davey. What did he say to you, exactly?"

London spilled her story, shaking her head as she recounted the night. Everything was okay until he told her he didn't like her job.

"Wait—he said he didn't like it or didn't like your job?"

"I don't know. Why does it matter? Is there a difference?"

"Actually, yes." Carrie sipped her wine. "I get it if he said he hated what you do, but it doesn't sound like that. It sounds to me that all he said was he didn't like you getting hurt. *That's* different."

London stared at her sister. Had she been so blinded by her anger that she misunderstood? It didn't matter. She'd stormed out, making a fool of herself. "It doesn't matter now. Even if that's true, I fucked up acting like a bitch."

"I dunno. I saw how Davey looked at you, London. Maybe you should call him."

"Or maybe you can just ask him." Alex smiled. "Because he just walked in with Uri."

"Shit." London turned to find Davey staring at her.

"Alex!" Uri called out as he walked towards them. "How's it hanging?"

"Cute, Uri. My tits don't hang... they're too perky for that."

Uri made a gagging sound. "Gross, Alex. I don't want to think about your tits."

"Hi, Davey." London cocked her head to the side. "Can we talk?"

"Sure. I'll catch you in a minute." Davey tipped his chin toward his friend and followed London towards the bathroom hallway.

"Look," she paced anxiously in front of him. "I'm sorry about the other night. I might have assumed something and reacted. It's just," her words were cut off by Davey's lips. He pressed her against the wall and ground into her.

When he pulled away, he was grinning. "You were saying?"

"Um… sorry about how I acted. Friends?" She held out her hand.

Davey stared at her hand for a moment. "Seriously, London?" Dave smiled as he pulled her against his chest. "I'll prove to you I'm not those guys. But you need to be sure you're ready for this." He motioned between them. "Until then, I'll give you space. You know where to find me." He pressed a kiss to her forehead and walked off.

What the fuck just happened?

London stood, rooted to the spot as he left her standing alone. When she finally walked back out to the bar, Carrie and Alex were laughing at something Uri was saying. Davey was tipping a beer to his lips as he watched her.

"Hey guys, I'll catch you later. I have to work tomorrow."

"Alright, sis. Stay safe." Carrie turned back to Uri.

"I'm sure we'll run into each other. We're on shift tomorrow." Alex pointed to herself, then the guys.

"Sure. See you around." London practically ran from the pub. She needed to think, and being in the same room with Davey was making it hard.

12

London barely slept. She couldn't shake his words. *"I'll prove to you I'm not those guys."* She didn't know how to take it. Was he saying that her job didn't bother him?

"Did you do anything exciting on your off days?" Frank coughed as he drummed his hands on the dashboard.

"Not really. Made an ass of myself… bout it. You?"

Frank turned toward her. "An ass of yourself? This sounds like an interesting story… what happened?"

"I might have overreacted to something, Davey said. Now I feel bad. That's all."

"Hurmpf." Frank grunted at me. "You're a stubborn woman. You've got to stop hiding behind the badge. You'll certainly pass up a good thing if you do."

"I know… anyway. How's Kathy? The kids?"

Frank smiled and filled the next few hours talking about his kids. The youngest was about to graduate from college, and he was damn proud. London couldn't help but be envious. Sometimes she wished she'd been a boy. Then she could have been a cop and had a family.

The sound of the radio broke their conversation. A domestic call, again. This time, the husband was possibly armed. London threw the siren on and headed towards the address dispatch had provided. Parking in the street, London and Frank headed towards the house. Using caution, London peered through the window and didn't see anyone inside.

"They sure this is the right address? I don't hear or see anyone."

Frank radioed in, confirming this was the location. London eased up the stairs to the front door. Frank stood to her right and carefully opened the glass door.

Just as London raised her hand to knock, a loud blast filled her ears. Searing pain scorched her body as she toppled over the porch railing.

"Signal 63... *OFFICER DOWN! OFFICER DOWN!*" she faintly heard Frank screaming into his radio.

Had he been shot?

London laid on the grass, staring into the sky. She heard more gunshots and screaming. She blinked, trying to pick herself up, but it felt like the weight of a thousand men were standing on her chest—she couldn't breathe. Her lungs burned as though someone had forced gasoline down her throat and lit a match.

"*London…*" She turned her head slightly as Frank knelt beside her. "FUCK…DISPATCH… WHERE THE FUCK IS THE AMBULANCE… London, please stay with me. I got you." Frank pressed his hand to her chest as she closed her eyes. Her whole body hurt.

DAVEY SAT ON THE COUCH NEXT TO ALEX. "SO, DAVEY." SHE smiled, "You and London?"

"Alex… let it go. Please."

"Look, Davey. She likes you, but London has had some really shitty guys in the past. If you want her, you'll have to work for it. But don't give up. I think you're good for her and vice versa. OK?" Just as he went to answer, the alarm bells sounded.

Station 19, respond to 1675 Baker Street. Signal 63.

Davey sucked in a breath and stood. "FUCK."

Alex beat him to the rig. "Let's go."

Davey jumped in and slammed his hands on the dashboard in frustration. He couldn't help the feeling something big was about to change his life—again.

Alex tried to sound confident, but even he could hear the uncertainty in her tone. "Davey—keep it together. We don't know who it is…"

"I just have a bad feeling. Can't you go faster?"

Alex sped through the intersection, nearly taking the light post down as she turned. As they pulled onto the street, Davey noted the flurry of activity. Emergency lights flashed, cop cars filled the road, and people were running around hollering.

Davey hopped out before the rig came to a complete stop. Alex hollered for him to slow down, but he kept moving, his legs pumping with pure adrenaline. Rounding a patrol car park haphazardly in the driveway, Davey nearly collapsed from the sight in front of him. Frank knelt beside London, pressing his uniform shirt to her chest. He'd stripped out of it to use it as gauze, and he was covered in blood… h*ers*.

He screamed out as he dropped to his knees beside them. *"WHAT THE FUCK!"*

Pulling the shirt back to expose the hole that adorned her chest, he fought down the vomit burning in his oesophagus. A hole where the bullet had gone in just below her collarbone glared at him from the edge of her vest. The vest was covered in blood, turning the once blue color a deep shade of brown.

"We hadn't even knocked. The fucker fired a shotgun through the door." Frank was fighting his emotions.

Alex dropped beside Davey, pulling equipment from her bag. "Help me get this off." She shoved scissors into his hands. "DAVEY!" She shouted, snapping him out of his haze.

Davey cut the remnants of her shirt and removed the Velcro straps of her vest. He cut the sides, lifting the chest plate off her body. Feeling for a pulse, he held his shit together and looked at his partner.

"Her pulse is thready. We have to get her on the stretcher and go, Alex."

"I know. Let me start a line." Alex hooked her up to an IV and hollered over her shoulder. Jason and Uri were at their side with the stretcher. Davey rolled her to her side, noting the bullet had gone clean through. He packed the hole with gauze and helped load her on the backboard. The guys helped him lift the stretcher in the back and Alex climbed inside with him. Jason slammed the doors shut and hollered as he climbed in the front, "I'm driving."

As they hooked her up to the heart monitor, her breathing stopped.

"FUCK. She's coding." Alex began chest compressions, pausing long enough for Davey to slap the defibrillator pads on her skin.

"Clear."

He pressed the button and watched as the machine jolted, causing her body to contort. They waited, watching the monitor. When nothing happened, Davey looked at Alex. "Nothing, push EPI."

Alex shoved the syringe into her arm and sat back as the machine jolted again. The steady sound of beeps filled the back of the rig.

"We got a pulse. Jason… GO Faster… we almost lost her." Alex slammed her hand onto the window of the ambulance, separating the front from the back.

Davey grabbed London's hand. "Don't you fucking die on me, London… DO you hear me?"

The short-lived sound of the machine ended as she coded again. Davey watched as the defibrillator shocked her repeatedly, but no heart waves appeared. He climbed onto the stretcher and started compressions. Silently praying for her to wake up. Davey continued, pressing her chest, not even aware he was being rushed into the ER.

"Son, I've got this." The ER Doctor gripped his hand and switched places as Davey slid off the bed. He watched as they disappeared behind closed doors.

Alex pressed her hand to his back. "Davey." He glanced over his shoulder at her. "Come on, let's go get cleaned up and then sit in the waiting room with the others."

Davey let her help him clean his hands up and then guide him through the doors towards a room full of people. His eyes found her sister Carrie, who was wrapped in the arms of an older man.

"DAVEY!" She screamed, running straight into his chest. She wrapped her arms around him, but he couldn't move. "How is she?"

Davey sucked in a breath, unable to hold his tears at bay. Memories of his dead fiancé Carley flooded his vision. Carrie gripped him as he practically collapsed to the floor. "Oh GOD... Is she...? Is she?"

Davey realised he hadn't answered her and steadied himself. Finally wrapping an arm around her, he guided them toward the others. "No... at least not yet. Come on, let's go sit down."

13

Davey sat, watching as members of the police department came and went. Frank had finally arrived and was looking rough.

"Frank?" Davey got up and move to sit down next to him.

He forced a smile. "So… you're the fella that has my partner all mixed up."

"I'm sorry?" Davey blinked.

"The paramedic, right? She likes you… a lot. And I think it may actually have her terrified."

"Terrified of what?"

Frank shrugged and smiled. "Love."

Davey shook his head. Love? What was this man talking about? They'd only been out a few times, and he wanted more, but love? Nah—Frank was mistake—right?

But as he sat there and listened to Frank talk about his partner with such adoration, he knew Frank was on to something. Somewhere in the short time he'd been around her, he'd gone and fallen in love with her.

"Fuck." He mumbled, pressing his hand to his forehead. "The last time we talked, I told her I'd let her figure things out. I walked away."

"She's tough. If anyone can pull through, it's her." Frank sucked in a breath, allowing the tears he held at bay to break free. "She's like a daughter to me. The best partner I've ever worked with. I'll say this… this won't change her mind about being a cop. Think you'll be able to handle that? Because if not, walk away now. She won't give up her career for any man." Frank eyed Davey.

Davey didn't speak. He didn't know what to say to Frank. He was about to open his mouth and speak, but the doctor burst through the doors. Her sister and father stood to greet him.

"Mr. Brett. Your daughter's out of surgery. She's being moved to ICU, but once she's settled, someone will come and get you."

"Doctor, is she alright?" Her father's voice was filled with hope. He motioned for him to sit down and took a seat across from him. "Mr. Brett, London, was shot through the chest. The bullet entered just below her collarbone at the edge of her left breast. It punctured a lung and shattered the clavicle when it entered. Her left shoulder blade was also fractured as the bullet exited. Now, I know she coded in the ambulance, but that was because of the amount of blood she lost. I won't lie—she will be in a lot of pain when she wakes up and will have a long recovery ahead of her. But." he smiled, "With some physical therapy, she will be back to full duty in a few months."

"Thank you." Her dad shook Davey's hand. Carrie pulled Davey into a hug. "Thank you. You saved her."

"I was just doing my job."

"No… it couldn't have been easy to work on someone you love, Davey."

"You love my daughter?" London's father looked at him in question.

"It's complicated."

"Uncomplicate it, son. You never know when you won't have the chance to repeat it."

Davey remained quiet. He knew exactly what it was like to not have the chance to say those words again. But was love what he was feeling?

"London Brett Family?" A nurse called out into the waiting room.

"That's us." Her sister hollered.

"Officer Brett is in the ICU. I can take her family back to see her now."

"Davey," Her dad smiled at me, "You and Carrie go back first. I'm not going anywhere, and I know you need to get back to the station."

"Are you sure?"

"Yes."

Davey shook Mr. Brett's hand before following Carrie towards the back. He knew she was going to look bad, but he wasn't ready for what he saw. She was wrapped up like a mummy, with tubes coming out of her sides and mouth.

"Why is she on a vent?" Carrie asked.

"The doctor felt with the punctured lung it was best to keep her in a medication-induced coma for 24 hours. It's just a precaution."

Carrie grabbed her hand and let out a sob. Davey rubbed Carrie's back and leaned down to press a kiss to London's head. "You get your ass well, London. We need to talk when you're awake."

Davey ran his knuckle down her face and pressed another kiss to her cheek. Seeing her so broken nearly broke him. He knew this was going to be the hardest thing she'd ever go through. As stubborn and strong-minded as she was, looking weak like this was going to make her crazy. He prayed she would let him help her. Deep down, he knew he would have a fight on his hands.

Kissing her one last time, he left her sister in the back alone. He bid farewell to her dad and Frank. Alex had gone back to see London but was running to catch up with him at the exit.

"Uri took the rig back for us. Chief took us out of service for the rest of the night. He said go home and had my car brought over. You need a ride?"

"Yeah, thanks."

Neither spoke as she drove. When she pulled up at his place, Davey climbed out and thanked her. He fell into his bed, exhaustion taking over as he fell asleep still fully clothed.

14

DAVEY ROLLED OVER, WIPING SLEEP FROM HIS EYES. AS THE FOG cleared, the events of the night before came rushing back to him.

London.

He sat up in bed, realizing he'd fallen into his covers, his clothes still covered in her blood. Jumping up, he stripped the sheets off and tossed them on the floor. Pulling his boots off, he shucked his pants and ripped his shirt over his head. He stormed into the bathroom and turned on the water. Stepping in, the sharp needles of the spray bit into his skin. Lathering his hands, he scrubbed the dried blood from his hands and arms. Pressing his hand to the tiles, he watched as the pink-tinged suds disappeared down the drain.

Closing his eyes, he thought about how close she'd come to death. Once he was sure he was clean, he turned off the spigot and stepped out. Wiping the fog covered window off with his hand, Davey stared at his reflection. His feelings terrified him. He'd sworn he'd never give his heart to anyone again… yet, here he was. Feeling lost and scared. He stepped into his room and grabbed his phone. He needed to talk to someone, so he called his sister.

"Davey! To what do I owe this pleasure?" Harley giggled on the other end.

"Harley." His emotions wavered, the stress of everything hitting him all at once.

Sensing something wasn't right in his tone, Harley grew serious. "Shit, Davey. What happened? Are you hurt?"

He cleared his throat. "No… I met someone. And,"

Harley cut him off. "That's great, but why do you sound like it's a bad thing?"

"She's a cop."

"Annnnnnddddd." Harley drew out, "that's bad. Why?"

"I worked a call last night. She was…" Davey pinched his temples. "She almost died."

"What? Oh my God, Davey. What happened?"

Davey told his sister everything—starting with their date and how it ended. When he was finished, there was silence on the other end of the call. "Harley?"

"Yeah… I'm here. Just processing what you told me. Do you love her?"

"I…" Davey smiled, "I don't know. It's too soon for that, right?"

"No. But that's not the real problem, is it?" Harley paused.

"What if she gets shot again? Or worse, dies? I don't know if I can handle another loss, Harley."

"Davey…" she sighed, "What happened to Carley was an accident. It could have just as easily been you or me. You can't go around avoiding a relationship because of a what-if."

"I hear you—but Harley, she's a cop. Her job is dangerous. Hell, she was shot, for fuck's sake."

"Right. But she didn't die. And from what it sounds like, she's good at her job despite what happened last night. You can't protect her from everything, Davey. You just have to trust she can protect herself. Hell, it could have been her partner instead of her. There's no way of knowing how things will play out. But hiding from love, that's just dumb."

Davey listened as she spoke. She was right about so many things. "How did you get so smart, Lil' sis?"

"Someone has to be smart in the family. By the way… did mom call you?"

"What's wrong with mom?"

"Nothing. Steven is coming home."

Davey couldn't hide how happy he was that his older brother, who'd been deployed for the last year, was coming home. "That's great. How long will he be home this time?"

"For good. He told mom he was ready to lay roots down. Whatever the hell that means."

Davey smiled. "That's awesome. Maybe you and he can come for a visit when he gets here."

Harley laughed. "Maybe he's home just in time for a wedding."

"Slow down… I haven't even told her I love her yet. Plus, she's not going to be happy having to be helped during her recovery. She's stubborn like someone else I know."

"Glad you're admitting it, big brother." Davey paused. He hadn't noticed what he slipped, but thinking about it more, he knew it was true. "Maybe that's why you love her. She reminds you of your favorite sibling."

"That must be it. Thanks, Harley. Tell mom and dad hi. And keep me posted on Steven."

"Love you, Davey. Go get your girl… will ya?"

"Alright. Love you too." Davey hung up and grinned. He missed his family but moving here had been just what he needed. Glancing at the clock, Davey decided to go to the hospital. He would sit by London's bed until he could talk to her.

Davey knew there was a chance she would reject him or, worse, tell him to leave. But he was done running from having a relationship. London was going to need someone to help her, and he intended that person to be him. Now he just needed to convince her. Davey slipped on some jeans and his department t-shirt.

Grabbing his keys, he smiled as he thought about her reaction. She was going to be pissed. London didn't want anyone taking care of her—it meant she was weak in her eyes. But she could never be that way to him. London was a goddamn rock star. And he planned to make sure she knew it.

15

The doctor had weaned her off the vent, feeling confident her lung was strong enough. Yet, she still hadn't woken up. The nurses assured Davey and Carrie that it was likely from the pain medication and to give her time. Davey paced her room like he was walking on hot coals.

Carrie had spent the last two nights in the hospital with London. "Davey, can you stop pacing? It's making me nuts."

"Sorry… I'm just frustrated that she hasn't woken up yet. I have to work tomorrow, and I was hoping she'd be awake before then." Davey stopped moving.

"I know me too. But the doctor says it takes everyone a different amount of time. She suffered a trauma… the body is trying to heal."

Davey smiled at her sister. Carrie was just as much a spitfire as she was—maybe more. "How the hell do your students deal with you?" In their time together, Davey learned Carrie was a middle school math teacher.

"They know when I am not playing. Now sit down. Did you hear from your brother yet?"

Davey had shared his brother was moving back stateside and that he was eager to hear from him. "No. Harley said he was due to return in a couple of weeks."

"Well, maybe you can introduce us. I am pretty sure we'll be family eventually, anyway."

"What makes you say that?"

"Please. You're in love with her… and I am pretty sure she feels the same. Even if she's scared."

A deep sigh and groan interrupted our conversation. "London." Davey ran to her side. "Hey, can you hear me?" He brushed a strand of hair from her face.

"Where am I?" Her voice cracked. "thirsty." She mumbled. Carrie ran out to get the nurse.

"London, do you know where you are?" Davey leaned down, getting eye level with her.

She forced her eyes open, taking in her surroundings. "Hospital?" She closed her eyes and let her head sink into the bed. "Why do I feel like I've been run over and I'm breathing in glass?"

"You were shot."

She sucked in a breath. "Fuck. I hurt."

"Miss Brett, Glad to see you're awake. You're in the hospital. Do you remember what happened?" The nurse began taking her vitals.

"Um… I don't…" She coughed, "FUCK!" She moaned.

"Yeah, that's going to hurt. Your lung was collapsed by the bullet."

"Bullet?" She glanced at Davey. "Frank? Oh god… is he… is Frank, ok?"

"He's fine. You were shot responding to a domestic. You almost died." The nurse dropped her hand. "I need to page the doctor. He will want to see you now that you're awake." She left the room, pulling the door shut.

"London. Do you remember what happened?"

London clenched her eyes closed, the sudden vision of memories flooding her head. She'd just lifted her hand to knock when she felt the heat tear through her body.

"I remember." A tear rolled down her cheek.

"Don't cry. You're alive. That's all that matters."

"How bad?" She glanced at Davey.

"Your clavicle was shattered, as well as your left shoulder blade. Aside from the punctured lung, you're in one piece. You'll gain full motion after some physical therapy."

"So, I still have a job?"

"Of course. Frank said they have you out on medical leave until cleared for duty."

"Ok." She closed her eyes. If she'd lost her career over this, she didn't know how she'd push forward. Hearing she'd get back to the road eventually made her relax. "How long?"

"How long what?" Carrie asked.

"How long will I be out of work?" London asked her sister.

Carrie was just about to answer, but the doctor came through the door. "Well, Miss Brett. I am glad to see you awake." He quickly assessed her and smiled. "You're coming along nicely."

"She just asked me how long she will be out of work." Carrie scoffed.

"Your injuries were significant. While you'll gain full mobility back, it's going to take some time. You'll need help getting around and someone to drive you to PT."

"How long?" She asked again, getting impatient.

"Most likely, two to three months."

London didn't speak. She simply closed her eyes and let the tears wash down her face. The doctor talked to Carrie and left the room. London still hadn't glanced at her sister or Davey. Her head was all jumbled up hearing she'd be out of work for two to three months. At some point, Carrie had left the room, leaving her and Davey alone.

"London." Davey sat on the edge of the bed. "Talk to me."

"I don't know what to say. My whole life has been turned upside down. And the last thing I need is to hear how you said my job was dangerous."

"I had no intention of saying anything."

"Right. You hate what I do. It's written all over you face every time I look at you. You know what? I need to be alone. Can you go?" London asked.

"You don't know what you're talking about, London."

"Davey. Please. Go." London turned her head away from him.

The bed shook as he stood. "I'll go, but we aren't done talking. You're wrong, London. I'm not looking at you because I think your job is dangerous. I'm looking at you, relieved because you didn't die." Davey stormed out, leaving London alone with the sound of the machines beeping. She was so confused and mad.

Mad at herself for what happened.

Confused about how he made her feel.

16

"Dude," Uri tossed an empty cup at Davey, "You look like shit."

Davey glanced up, finding his fellow firemen staring at him. He hadn't slept well the last few nights. Not since London kicked him out of her hospital room. Alex had been by to visit her a few times and told him she just needed some space, but Davey couldn't help being hurt. He needed to see her.

Davey needed to put a different image in his head—other than the one of her lying on the ground bleeding out. When he thought he'd lost her in the back of the ambulance, his heart plummeted. After Carley died, Davey swore he'd never give his heart to another, out of fear of breaking it again, and when her heart stopped… so did his.

"Earth to Davey." Alex called out to him. "Uri was asking you a question."

"What?" Davey shook the mental image of her from his head. "You said something?"

"Yeah, man. I said you looked like shit and then asked if you'd seen her."

"She doesn't want me there."

Alex scoffed, "You're an idiot."

"What? She told me to leave, and when I went back the next day, Carrie told me she didn't want to see me. How does that make me an idiot?"

"Davey…" Alex pinched the bridge of her nose, "London is an alpha female. As long as I've known her, she puts on this front of being strong. She thinks because she is in a man's world, she can't be needy. It's an act. I know deep down she wants to have it both ways. Someone to hold her and take care of her—and then the tough, macho version when she is in uniform. The problem is, no man has handled that. They all try to change her. Make her feel less. And now," She drew in a breath. "Now… she's been knocked down. She almost died. I am going to go out on a limb and say she feels like she isn't in control, and it probably freaks the shit out of her to need someone. And trust me, she needs someone bad. My question to you is… Are you strong enough for her? Can you help her see you can support her and still let her have room to fly? If not, then you definitely need to stay away."

The alarm sounded, ending the conversation. As they climbed into the ambulance, Davey couldn't help hearing Alex's words replay in his head. Was he strong enough to be that man? Squeezing his eyes shut, Davey pushed the confusion to the back and focused on his job. For now, he just needed to be a paramedic.

The shift blew by with boring calls. For once, Davey was grateful. He wasn't really in a place to think about anything serious. London consumed his thoughts too much. As he was climbing into his truck, his phone rang. Glancing at the screen, he smiled.

"Harley, how's it going?"

His sister's shrill scream echoed through his truck. "DAVEY! HE'S HOME!!!"

"What? Steven's there?"

"YES!" She blew out a breath. "Sorry. His plane just landed, and he called mom as soon he got off. He should be here in about an hour. Are you coming home?"

Davey thought about it for a minute. "You know what? I am. I just got off shift, and I need to getaway. Steven coming home is the perfect excuse to make the drive. Give me a few hours and I'll be there."

"YES! Mom will be so happy to have you home, Davey. We've missed seeing you."

"I know, but you understand this is where I need to be, right?"

Her voice softened. "Of course. How's London?"

"Fine, I guess." Dave grumbled at the reminder the woman he loved was avoiding him.

"You guess? Davey, did something happen?"

"Yeah… look." Davey put his truck in gear. "I don't want to talk about it. I'll see you in a few hours. Love you, sis."

Davey disconnected, not wanting to explain what he was feeling right now. Harley would hound him about it. She could get like a dog going after a bone with some things. Putting everything out of his head, Davey hurried home and changed. He threw a small duffle bag in his truck. Knowing he didn't have to be back on shift for two days, he planned to spend some time with his family.

17

LONDON FELT LIKE HER WHOLE BODY WAS ON FIRE. EVERY breath was like a shard of glass piercing her ribs. The doctor warned her it would be painful the first couple of days, but this was more than unpleasant—It was pure hell. She caught her father looking at her as she sat in the chair close to her bed.

"What, dad?" London barked. She was tired of being so helpless, and having her dad look at her as though she was fragile made her cringe.

"London. You nearly died. If I want to stare at you and be thankful you're not, then I will."

London closed her eyes, "I'm sorry, dad. I just hate being so helpless. And I fucking hurt!" She let out a sob. Her dad moved to sit by her on the bed. He pressed his hand to her forehead and brushed her hair back.

"I know. You've always been a stubborn girl. Even when you were little, if we said you couldn't do something, you'd prove us wrong. But London," he smiled at her, "You need to learn sometimes you need help. Sometimes you need someone to lean on. You can't always be this tough cop. Even I know sometimes you need that person to help you. Your mother was that person to me. And when she died, you and Carrie became that person. It's ok to be vulnerable."

"Dad," London let the tears spill on her face.

"You shouldn't push people who love you away. It's not healthy, and you'll end up an alone old spinster."

"Are you saying I'm a spinster?"

"No. Not yet." London smiled even through the pain. Her dad was the greatest man she knew. He supported her wish to be a cop and pushed her to work hard.

"You know," He stood and walked toward the door, "Davey asks about you every day. I like him. He's a good man. I'll leave you to rest and think about what I've said. I love you, baby girl." He pushed through the door, leaving her to her thoughts. Just a week ago, she was near death. Now she laid confined to the bed wishing the pain would ebb somehow.

"London?" Her doctor walked in, smiling as she forced a smile in return. "How are you feeling today?"

"Like I've been shot." She retorted.

"Yes. I imagine you do. Now let's have a look at you." He poked and prodded her in places she'd rather he not. After listening to her chest, checking her eyes, and inspecting the bandages, he smiled. "Well, you are healing well. Your lungs sound good, all things considering. I imagine you're tired of being cooped up in this room."

"You have no idea." London's snarky tone slipped from her mouth, "Sorry. It's just hard relying on others so much."

"Well, get used to it for a while. You're going to need help with basic things for at least eight weeks."

"Basic things? What do you mean?"

"For starters, showering. You cannot get this area saturated. A little wet is one thing, but soaked, no. And dressing will be a challenge. You cannot raise your arm above your head or pull up your own pants. Not without damaging your shoulder more or ripping stitches. So, relying on someone is needed."

"Great." London closed her eyes.

"But, on the upside, if your x-rays come back clear, which I suspect they will, you will be released. What do you think?"

"Wait—like released, released?"

"As long as you have someone at home to help with your care, then yes."

"Thank you!" London smiled, wincing in pain as she reacted.

"See, you need someone to rein you in, so you don't do more damage. And of course, someone to drive you to physical therapy."

"I forgot about that. How long is that sentence?"

"Depends on you, but likely twelve weeks."

"Three months?"

"Yep. Now, if you'll excuse me, I am going to put in the request for your scan. Let me know if you need anything else."

"Thank you, doctor." London dropped her head to the pillow again, mentally screaming about being helpless. Maybe Carrie would come to stay with her for a little while. She didn't want to move back home. As soon as Carrie came by, London would ask her. Giving in to the pain meds, London let sleep claim her.

18

Davey's chest constricted with emotions he wasn't prepared to feel as he pulled into his parent's driveway. He'd been back to visit a few times since leaving his hometown, but this time it felt different. Sitting behind the steering wheel of his truck, he stared blankly at the house in front of him. His sister's face in the driver's window startled him from memories he didn't want to face.

"Davey! You going to sit out here all day or come inside?" She tapped on the window, smiling.

"Yeah—coming." He climbed from the seat and slammed the door. Pulling Harley into a hug, "Good to see you, sis."

Harley pulled back and held his stare. "Come inside. Steven will be glad to see you. We can talk later about what's bothering you."

"Nothing's bothering me."

"You can't lie to me, Davey." She tugged his elbow towards the house. "But I'll let you have your secrets for now."

When he stepped through the front door, the shrill scream of his mom had him shaking his head.

"DAVEY!" She pulled him into a tight embrace. "It's so good to have everyone home."

Davey chuckled, "Where's Steven?"

Releasing her son, "In his room. He's…" she drifted off, her shoulders drooping "… tired, I guess."

"Mom. It can't be easy coming home. Give him time to adjust to civilian life. You making dinner?"

"Of course!" she padded off towards the kitchen.

"Son." His dad emerged from the hallway. "Glad you came. Steven will be glad to see you."

"Thanks, dad." Davey shook his hand and hugged him. "I'll pop back and see him."

Stopping in front of his brother's childhood door, Davey took a deep breath. It had been years since he'd seen his brother. The last time, he and Carley were just engaged.

"Steven," Davey rapped on the door as he pushed inside and closed it behind him.

"Davey." Steven stood, seemingly unsure of how to respond to Davey. "I'm sorry I wasn't here."

Davey tugged him into his arms. "Don't. You were off saving the world."

"That's no excuse. You're my brother, and I didn't even come home when you needed me."

Davey looked at his brother. Years of being entrenched in war had taken its toll on him. His face was hardened, and the shine in his eyes held had tempered to a dull glare. When Carley died, Davey had been angry that Steven didn't come home. But seeing him here, worn and changed, Davey regretted those feelings.

"It's the past. You're here now, and that's all that matters."

Steven nodded. "How are you doing? Dad said you transferred to Clinton."

"Yeah. I needed a change—a fresh start."

"Did you get one?" Steven smiled.

"Harley told you?"

"She just mentioned you met someone. You deserve to be happy, Davey. Carley would have wanted that."

"Well… I'm not sure that's in the plan."

"Sounds like you need a beer. I know I do."

"Mom has dinner. Let's eat, then go grab one. We can catch up."

"Harley will want to come." Steven brushed his short hair back with his hand.

"That's fine. I might need a female's perspective, anyway."

CARRIE STARED AT HER SISTER. "YOU WANT ME TO WHAT? London…" She huffed out a frustrated breath, "I love you, but I can't move in with you. I have a job—remember?"

"Carrie," she winced as she sat up, "I am aware of that. But I can't be alone, and I don't want to move in with dad."

"Fuck me. You are really making this hard."

"Making what hard?" Alex smiled as she walked into London's room.

"She wants me to move in and help her with recovery. I love you, London, but no. I'm sorry. There has to be another way."

"There's not. The doctor said I've got to have someone at home to help me before he releases me. Please, Carrie?"

"You can come to my place, but I am not moving to yours. Even for a few weeks."

"You seriously expect me to walk up four floors to your apartment? I can't even get to the bathroom ten feet away because my lungs feel like I'm making diamonds in them."

"I can come for a few days, but not weeks."

"That's not going to help…" London screamed in frustration.

"What if I came and stayed with you?" Alex finally spoke.

"Seriously?" London looked at her friend.

"Yeah. I mean, someone would have to stay the nights I worked at the station, but I don't mind. Hell, it'd be nice to have a roommate again." Alex smiled.

"Oh, my God. Are you serious? Alex, you would be a lifesaver."

The doctor walked in. "So… London, did you get something worked out? Your scans came back great, which means as long as you have home help, you can go home tomorrow."

"Doc…, my sweet friend, has agreed to stay with me during recovery. And she's a paramedic, so I'd say I have it perfectly worked out."

He glanced at the tiny woman standing at the end of the bed. "I'd say you have it worked out well." His voice made everyone blush. "Ms…" he paused.

"Boatman. Alex Boatman. I work at Station 19."

"Doctor Blake Williams." He stuck his hand out to shake Alex's hand. "But please, call me Blake. I've seen you come in with the rig. Can you come with me so we can discuss how to best help London?"

"Um… sure. London, I'll be back in a few."

Carrie stood slack jaw as she watched Alex follow the doctor from the room. Neither she nor London spoke, but as soon as the door closed, both erupted into laughter.

"Oh, God…" London clutched her side, "It hurts to laugh."

"That man is totally into her. Think she realizes it?" Carrie snorted.

"Think we should tell him she probably likes the nurses more?"

Carrie laughed again. But her laughter died, and she grew serious as she turned to her sister. "London, I'm sorry I told you no. But…"

London cut her off. "I know. It was wrong of me to ask you to uproot your whole life. I just knew I couldn't make it up your stairs."

"How about I come when Alex is at work?"

"Thanks." London gave a half-smile. Considering Alex's work made her think about Davey.

"Why don't you just call him London?"

"I can't. He already said he hated my job—and then I went and got shot. I won't be with a man who doesn't support what I love."

"I saw him. He was haunted by what happened to you… but it was more than that. He thought he'd lost you."

"It doesn't matter. I told him to leave, and he hasn't come back or called. That says it all."

"I still think you're wrong. But I'll drop it for now."

19

"You've been staring at that beer like it's going to drink itself." Steven motioned towards the half-empty glass Davey held in his hand. "What's got you so twisted up, brother?"

"A woman has him twisted up," Harley laughed as she ordered another drink.

"Shut up, Harley." Davey nursed his beer.

"She must be some woman to have you fucked up like this. What's the problem?"

"She's a cop."

"And?" Steven smirked at him. "You have an issue with that?"

"No… yes… I don't know. It's complicated."

"What's complicated about it? Lots of women have tough jobs. Hell, I had women on my team in Afghanistan that did a better job than some of the men."

"I don't like that she could get hurt… again." Davey swallowed the rest of the amber liquid and signaled the bartender for another.

"You… of all people should know that it doesn't matter what you do in life, there's no way to stop someone from getting hurt."

Davey looked at his brother. "That was low."

"Doesn't make it any less true. I lost a lot of friends overseas—but it doesn't mean I want to hole up and stop living."

"I didn't think I could love after Carley. When she died, it ripped a hole in my chest that has slowly been draining my life. Moving to Clinton was supposed to help me find a way to live without her memory haunting me."

"No, it wasn't," Harley spoke. "It was a way for you to run away. Davey—you haven't even been to Carley's grave since her funeral. I'm not even sure you remember the service. You were in such a daze."

"I couldn't go back, Harley."

"Maybe it's time. Maybe you should go say goodbye to the demons, keeping you from living again, brother. Carley would want you to have a life."

"How does that help me in my current situation?"

"You can't truly move on until you let go of the past. I think deep down, you know this girl can take care of herself. It's not her job stopping you from pursuing her. It's you."

Steven's words rattled around in his head. Was he right? Was it his past that held him in fear? Davey knew London was tough.

Hell, he'd seen her take down a man twice her size with a knife. That's what he loved about her. She wasn't afraid of anything.

Fuck.

The realization hit him like a ton of bricks. He was in love with her. When he saw her bleeding out on the ground, his world stopped moving. Closing his eyes, he pushed his stool back and stood. "I need to go. Can you catch a ride back with Harley?"

"You're realizing I'm right?" Harley laughed.

"There's something I need to do first. Tell mom I'll be back later. And Harley," Davey turned towards his sister, "Thanks. Uri, I'm glad you're home." With that, Davey turned and left the bar.

He pulled alongside the small drive. Davey hadn't been here since he buried Carley. Taking a deep breath, he climbed out of his truck. The sky had faded into a rosy pink as the sun began to set. But putting this off because of the time of day would be another excuse to avoid coming. Davey flinched as the door slammed beneath his hand. Frozen, he stared towards the spot that held his first love. His only love until now. Kneeling into the dirt, he rested his hand on the gravestone.

"Carley. I came. I know it's been a while. I just couldn't bring myself to come back. It made it less real. I could tell myself you were on an extended trip and would come back one day. But I know that was foolish."

Davey sat down, resting his elbows on his knees. "You were the woman I was supposed to spend eternity with. We had plans. That day they told me you were gone, a part of me died. I was numb. Hell, a part of me is still numb. But I met someone. And for the first time in a while, I felt alive. It's silly, really. We've only known each other for a few weeks, but I can't stop thinking about her. I feel guilty. I shouldn't feel this way about another woman—right? You were supposed to be it for me. I think you would like her. She's different from you. Maybe that's why I'm drawn to her. Her name is London. And man, is she feisty. The thing is, I love her, Carley. But I'm scared. She's a cop—and her job is dangerous. Hell, she was shot last week, and I almost lost her before I even really have her. It scares me to give my heart, knowing I could lose it again. I wish you were here. I wouldn't be having this conversation because we'd be together. But life didn't work out that way. I never told you goodbye. And I guess it's part of what keeps me stuck in fear."

Davey pushed off the ground and dusted his pants off. "But living in fear isn't living. I love you, Carley. You'll always be a part of my heart. The thing is… I think I'm ready to give what's left away." Davey rested his hand on Carley's headstone. "I love you, Carley-bear." Davey turned and walked out of the cemetery. He knew it was time to move forward. And if he had his way, it would be with a stubborn woman in blue.

20

It had been two days since Davey said goodbye to Carley, and he felt as though a weight had been lifted from his soul. He still hadn't called London. He wanted to respect her wishes, but he wouldn't wait much longer to go to her.

"How was your time away from the station, Davey?" Uri smacked his boot.

"Good. My brother is home from the military, so I went home to see him."

"Wow… that's awesome. Hey, I heard your girl was released."

"What?" Davey looked at his friend. "She at home?"

Alex plopped into the seat in front of him. "Yep."

"I hope her sister moved in for a little while. She shouldn't be alone."

Alex shook her head. "Nope. Carrie wouldn't move in."

Davey jumped out of his seat, ready to storm over to London's house. "What the fuck?"

"Calm down. I'm staying with her." Alex patted his shoulder. "And when I'm on shift, Carrie stays there."

He eyed his friend. "You're staying with her?"

"Yeah… you have a problem with that?"

"Yes." Davey glared at his partner. "You can go home after shift, Alex."

"Um. No. I'll be going to her house as planned."

"It's unnecessary. I'll be going over there to take care of her." Davey pushed past his partner and stormed out of the room.

Alex looked at Uri. "What the fuck just happened?"

"Love will fuck with your head, Alex. I wouldn't get in his way if I were you." Uri's head shook with his laughter.

"Love… Davey loves her?"

Uri turned toward the door that Davey darted through. "Yeah. I think he does."

Alex followed Uri's line of sight. "Shit. Guess I better call Carrie."

LONDON LAID IN HER BED, STARING AT THE CEILING. SHE'D BEEN awake since the sun started peeking through her blinds. Carrie came in to tell her she was off to work and that her relief would be there in an hour. Glancing at her clock, she knew Alex should be there soon. Slipping her feet from under the covers, she pressed her feet to the wooden floor. Her house was modest, but hers. She'd bought it shortly after graduating from the police academy. She padded her way into the bathroom and glanced at her reflection. Her hair was matted to the side of her face. Turning to the shower, she turned the water on hot.

"What the hell are you doing?" The deep, timbre voice she hadn't heard in weeks startled her.

"What the FUCK!" She winced as she jumped, turning to find Davey standing in the doorway of her bathroom. "Davey… how did you get into my house?"

He held up a key. "The front door. Now, why would you try to shower alone? You know it's not safe."

London flicked the water off. "Where's Alex?"

"I sent her home."

"Home?" London padded by him and sat on her bed. "You sent Alex home?"

"Yep. Now, do you need a shower or not?" Davey walked towards her.

"Why are you here, Davey?"

"Because you can't be alone… and I can't stay away."

London sucked in a breath. "I can do this alone. Go home. Never mind. Tell Alex, I'll be fine."

Davey kneeled in front of London. "You're a strong woman. No…" he pulled her hands into his. "You're badass. But you were shot, and now you need someone to help you heal. Let me be that person."

"Why?"

"London," Davey stood and paced in front of her. His back was to her as she watched him run his fingers through his hair. "When we got the call that an officer was down… everything stopped. And then I saw you on the ground bleeding. Your heart stopped in the rig, and so did mine. For the last few years, I've been avoiding life. When my fiancé died, part of me died with her. Then I met you. You're unlike any woman I've ever met. You're fearless and work hard. And there's a part of you I think loves just as hard. But you've never found someone you trust enough to give your heart to. Until me." Davey turned to face her. "I don't care what you do for a living… as long as you come home to me—you could be an astronaut for all I care. Now… how about that shower?"

London's world tilted as she listened to Davey talk. "I don't know what to say." She whispered, more to herself than to him.

Say nothing right now. But know this… I'm not leaving. I took a couple of weeks off from the station."

"What… no. You can't stay here."

"It's not up for debate. I already talked to Carrie, your dad, and Alex."

"I'm going to kill them."

Davey walked over and scooped her up gently. "Let's get you showered."

London sucked in a breath. "You can't be serious. Put me down."

Davey ignored her as he walked her into the bathroom and turned the water back on. The room filled up with steam as he sat her down on the toilet. He started unbuttoning her shirt.

"Hold up. You cannot undress me, Davey." But even as she spoke the words, she knew she didn't want him to stop. Him being here scared the shit out of her. But it also made her heart warm. Davey simply smiled and tugged her shirt off.

He closed his eyes as if he was praying. "You alright?"

"Yes… it's just the first time—" his words drifted off, making London realize he hadn't seen her scars since he responded to the call of her being shot.

London gripped his hand. "I'm fine."

Davey traced the bandage along her shoulder. His finger moved the path down to her breast and back up to her neck. His fingers moved to the back of her neck as he pulled her face toward him. He rested his forehead against hers. "London…" his breath tickled her lips just as he claimed her lips. His kiss was gentle, even as he slipped his tongue into her mouth.

When he broke the kiss, he simply smiled. London didn't speak. She didn't know what to say. Davey confused the hell out of her. She'd told him to leave in the hospital, yet here he was.

Breaking her from her thoughts, he tugged her to stand. "Let's get you up."

He squatted in front of her and slid her pants down her legs. Davey guided her into the shower, removing the handheld shower head. "Let me help you."

He grabbed a loofa and began washing her body with a tenderness that left London shaking. "Lean your head back."

Following his command, she relaxed as he washed her hair, keeping the water from her bandage. Once he finished, he cut the water off and wrapped her in a towel. Scooping her off her feet once more, Davey carried her to the bed. He helped her slip into some leggings and eased a fresh button-up shirt on. "Now. Let me get you something to eat so you can take your medication. Lay down, I'll be right back."

London propped herself against her pillows and watched as Davey left the room. She felt like she was in some sort of dream. Part of her was angry that he was here, seeing her so vulnerable, and wished it wasn't real. The other part of her hoped if she was dreaming that she stayed asleep and didn't wake up—and that scared her.

21

London didn't know what to think. Davey had been there to help her through her recovery. When he was on shift, her sister stayed with her. They never spoke about Davey—Carrie avoided the topic like the plague. Now, nearly a month later, she didn't know why they were still at her house. Her doctor had told her at the two-week check-up she could start back to a semi-normal routine as long as she took it easy with her arm. Her lung was fully healed, and it no longer felt like breathing glass. When she'd told Davey and Carrie that they didn't have to stay with her any longer, they'd both laughed.

This only confused London more. Her body was mostly healed —not really, but she liked to make herself think it was. Being helpless was going against everything she was. Her job as a police officer was all she cared about. Even as the thought entered her head, her eyes found Davey gathering laundry. The scene was so domestic.

"I can do my own laundry, Davey," London called after him as she followed him into the tiny space that held her washer and dryer.

"The doctor was clear on you not doing anything to strenuous for the first couple of weeks." He spoke without looking at her as he tossed her delicate into the washer and shut the lid.

"Maybe I don't want you touching my things. It's weird."

"Trust me, this is not how I wanted my hands on your panties. But it's necessary. Now," he turned to face her, "Are you ready?"

London froze. His body was so close to hers; she could feel the heat radiating off him. The electricity that was flowing between them was undeniable. London sucked in a breath. "Ready for what?" she whispered.

Davey's laugh caused her to jump. "Your doctor's appointment and physical therapy."

"Oh." London backed out of the room, Davey closely following. She winced as she backed into the wall.

"Shit." Davey pulled her towards him, searching her body as he spun her too look her over. "Be careful, London."

"I'm fine. And yeah… I'm ready."

Davey grabbed her good arm and guided her out of the house. He hoisted her into his truck and slid into the driver's seat.

"London," Davey paused, closing his eyes. He wanted to tell her what he was feeling, but he knew she wasn't ready to hear it yet. The last few weeks had been pure torture for him. He'd promised he wouldn't pursue her until she was ready, but damn, every time she got close to him, the sexual tension made him want to shove her against the closest surface and have his way with her.

But one wince from her reminded him why that couldn't happen. She was still recovering. "Buckle up." He threw the car in drive and took them to her doctor's office.

Today was her four-week check-up. London started physical therapy two weeks ago, and her therapist was a brutal woman. She told her it wouldn't be easy if she wanted full motion in her arm again. Davey was in the waiting room, but part of her wanted him back here with her. Shaking her thoughts from her head, she smiled at the doctor as he walked in.

"Ms. Brett. How's my favorite patient?"

"Cute, Doc. You know I've probably been a nightmare."

"Nonsense, now. Let's have a look."

He did his routine checks and then grabbed her arm. "I want to see your flexibility. You ready?"

"Um… Sure." London smiled. That expression leaving her lips as soon as he pulled her arm up overhead. She thought the physical therapist was a masochist, but this was a whole new level.

"What the fuck?" she gritted out as he moved and bent her arm, applying steady pressure on her shoulder blade.

"You're healing nicely. I know it hurts, but your range of motion is remarkable. In fact, I'd say you're ready to go back to light duty if you want."

London thought she misunderstood. "What did you say?"

"I said you're ready to return to work—light duty."

"Oh, my GOD! Yes… *Please…*" London didn't hide the tears, misting her eyes, "Thank you."

"Don't thank me. You're a fighter, Ms. Brett. You've obviously been following directions and doing what you should to allow this to happen. Now don't do something stupid and try to lift anything heavy or do push-ups. But if you feel up to it, you can start exercising again. It would do your lungs good. Nothing too strenuous. Talk with your therapist—he will guide you well."

"Thank you. You have no idea how this makes me feel."

"Stop at the desk, and my nurse will get you the needed paperwork. See you in another two weeks. Call me if you have any issues. Otherwise, you're clear for normal activities."

London walked from the room, beaming. She grabbed the needed papers and met Davey in the waiting room. He stood as she entered.

"I take it that the visit went well." His voice was deep and sent shivers straight to her core.

"Very well. I've been cleared for light-duty and normal daily activity. Can we stop by the station after therapy?"

Davey sucked in a breath. He knew this day was coming. He just hoped he'd have more time. "Sure. I guess that means you don't need me to stay at your place anymore."

London could hear the sadness lacing his statement. "Davey. I can't thank you enough for helping me the last month. Although you never told me why you stayed, and Alex didn't." She raised an eyebrow, waiting for his response.

"I wasn't going to let anyone else ensure your safety." He walked out the door, leaving her to ponder his words.

"Wait…" she hurried to catch up with him, "What does the mean?"

Davey opened the door and helped her in. "Exactly what it sounds like, London."

Neither spoke as he drove his truck to her next appointment. He wasn't ready to tell her what he was feeling, and she wasn't prepared to push him for more.

22

THE HOUSE WAS EERILY SILENT AS LONDON WALKED INTO THE kitchen. She sat at the bar and drank a cup of coffee. Today was the first day back to work. It wasn't on patrol, but it was something. Straightening her polo shirt beneath the sling, she was required to wear London grabbed her keys and opened the front door. She was shocked to see Davey standing on the other side.

"Davey?" she stepped out, pulling the door closed and locking it. "What are you doing here?"

"I wanted to wish you good luck." That's when London caught sight of the ambulance parked on her curb, Alex waving from the passenger seat.

"You came by on duty?"

"Yep. Come on, I'll walk you to your car."

London stopped walking. "You didn't have to come here, Davey. I don't understand."

Davey opened her driver's door. "I just needed to make sure you were ok."

"I'm fine. But I need to get going—maybe you and Alex can meet me for lunch." She eased herself into her car when Davey wrapped his arm around her waist, stopping her.

"What…" her words died on her lips as he pressed his to them. The kiss was gentle at first, but soon she leaned into him, and it became more than innocent.

Davey pulled away. "Good luck on your first day back, London." He turned and bolted to the rig, waiting for him. She pressed her fingers against her swollen mouth and watched as the ambulance eased off the curb. Finally, blinking from her daze, she slipped into the seat. It was a challenge to buckle herself in, but after managing it, she cranked the car. For what felt like an eternity, she simply sat staring at the steering wheel. She didn't know what to think of Davey's sudden appearance and the kiss. Backing out slowly, London found herself smiling and confused. A combination that left her uneasy.

"You really do like her, don't you?" Alex asked from the seat next to him. Davey planned on just stopping by and wishing her luck. The kiss had been spontaneous.

"More than that, Alex."

Alex eyed her partner as he stared through the windshield. "You mean that, don't you?"

"Yes."

"I thought you didn't do relationships."

"I didn't either. But then my brother made some valid points when I went home a while back. And my sister Harley pointed out the only thing stopping me was me. So, I did something I swore I wouldn't do."

"What's that?" Alex questioned, curious about what finally knocked some sense into her friend.

"I said goodbye to the past."

Alex said nothing for a few minutes. She simply stared at Davey. "What does that mean, though, Davey? You know she will only accept you if you can handle both sides of her."

"She could be anything she wants, Alex. I'd still feel the same way. Her job doesn't matter to me. She does."

"Wow—have you told her this?"

"No. She's afraid… I can feel it. I am giving her time to heal and get back to duty. Only then will I be able to show her it doesn't matter to me. She's a cop."

"I'm impressed. I think you're an idiot for not saying something, but I get it… I think." She smiled at him.

"It's been damn hard not to act on my desire for her—but now that I'm not living in the house with her, it's been easier. I'm going to show her she can trust me and let her be the one to come to me."

"And if she doesn't?"

"She will… and I am a patient man. I'll wait."

"This is going to be fun to watch."

Davey grumbled, "What's that supposed to mean?"

"You're both stubborn. She won't give in without a fight, and you're going to die trying to wait. I can't wait to tell the guys about this." Alex jumped out of the rig when they pulled back into the station. Davey sighed as he watched his partner practically run inside. Maybe he shouldn't have told her his plans or his feelings. She could laugh all she wanted—Davey was going to make London his. And if Alex was right, that he'd probably die trying, well… at least he'd die a happy man.

23

"LONDON!" Frank bellowed as he rounded the corner and caught sight of her sitting at the front desk. "God, you're a sight for sore eyes. You didn't tell me you were coming back today."

"I wanted to surprise you." She stood, giving her long-time partner a side hug. "How's it going with your new partner?" The words hurt as she said them.

"Not new. Temporary. And he's an idiot." Frank bellowed, "He actually tried to get me to eat tofu at some health nut lunch place. Can you believe that?"

"It probably wouldn't hurt you, Frank."

"Hurt me? What the fuck is tofu anyway… no, thank you. I didn't get to my age to eat rabbit food."

London didn't realize how much she missed being here. Frank and his wife Kathy had visited her many times over the last month, but this was different. It felt like being home.

"So," Frank propped himself against the desk, "How's the roomie?" He waggled his eyebrows.

"Stop, Frank. He's just a friend."

"You keep telling yourself that… but I know that look a man gets when he's fallen. And that boy has fallen hard."

"Nah… he had his love once. She died. He said he'd never do that again."

"You're really daft, London." Frank's belly rumbled with laughter. The sound echoing through the empty lobby.

"Daft?" London shook her head. "Are you sure you weren't shot, Frank? Geez." As she smiled at her friend, a teenage girl came into the lobby carrying a huge bouquet of roses.

"Can I help you?" London smiled.

"I have a delivery for a…" the girl glanced at her clipboard, "London Brett."

"That's me." She took the flowers and signed for them.

"Have a great day." The girl winked and skipped out of the department.

"Well… What do we have here?" Frank tried to snatch the card from London.

"Stop. It's probably from my dad." London opened the card, deep down, knowing it wasn't her dad's style.

London,

I hope your first day back is all you thought it'd be.

Davey

"From your dad?" Frank peered over her shoulder, trying to read the card.

"No. Davey." London tucked the card back into the tiny envelope and shoved it into her pocket.

"Still think he's just a friend?"

"Yes… ugh… I dunno." She put her head into her hands. "What am I supposed to do, Frank?"

"Stop running away from your feelings." Frank patted her back. "You are so focused on being tough, you don't give yourself a chance to be anything else."

"I don't understand."

"London, when's the last time you were in love?"

"Love… I don't know. I guess never. Men don't love women like me. They like the idea of what they think they can turn me into. But they don't love all of me."

"Something tells me you're wrong about this one. Anyway, I gotta go. Who knows what this tree hugger of a partner is doing… London," Frank glanced at her before walking off, "Stop running."

London sat at the desk, thinking about what Frank said. *Did* she run? She wasn't afraid of many things, but the thought of opening her heart to someone, just to be disappointed, scared the ever-loving shit out of her. She would just keep focusing on recovering. The sooner she could get back to full duty, the better she would be.

24

After a long shift, Davey decided he would stop by London's house. She would be getting ready to head into work, so he knew he'd be able to catch her as she was leaving. Pulling his truck to the curb, he cut the engine and just sat there. He wanted to show her she didn't need to hide from the energy they shared. Davey was scared, too. Hell, the last few years he'd hidden away from anything close to a romantic attachment. A few flings here and there to sedate his carnal needs were no longer enough. One night in her bed, and he knew she was it for him. As she stepped out the door, Davey hurried from his truck to meet her at her car.

"Morning, London."

"Davey," his name sounding breathless as he neared her. "What are you doing here? Didn't you work last night?"

"Yes—just getting off and wanted to see you."

"Oh," London ran her hands through her hair nervously. "I got your flowers. Thank you."

"How was your first day back?"

"Boring, but good. It's hard just sitting behind the desk when I want to be out in the car with Frank." London watched for his reaction.

"I bet. But you'll be back out there before you know it."

She shifted nervously. "I hope so. Thanks for stopping by again. I have to go through. I have therapy before going into the station."

"Sure. I just wanted to see you." Davey smiled.

London took a deep breath. "Would you like to come for dinner later? I feel like I owe you for taking care of me."

"Sure, I'll bring some wine." His smile took the air from her lungs.

"Great. I'll text you when I am headed home later. See you tonight, Davey." London got into her car, but he pulled her to him once again, and pressed his lips to hers.

"See you tonight," he mumbled before turning and disappearing into his truck.

London was so flustered as she got in her car. What was happening? Everything in her body screamed to run in the opposite direction, but her heart pleaded with her to stay. She was going crazy. She didn't remember the drive to the therapist's office, only when she pulled into a parking space did London realize she was there.

"Shit." She swore as she got out of the car. Davey had a way of making her forget everything around her. She needed to talk to

Carrie or Alex. London's head was swirling with confusion when she stepped into the office.

"London," the receptionist called her name, "Felicity's waiting for you."

"Thanks." She smiled as she headed back to the torture chamber.

"Morning, Felicity." London smiled as she set her keys and phone down.

"London, you're looking quite cheery this morning." Her grin was kind. But London knew that just meant she was going to create pain like she'd never felt before.

"I don't like that look, Felicity."

"You know me too well. Now, tell me what you has grinning like the Cheshire cat."

London took her seat on the bench as Felicity began stretching her arm. "Nothing. I'm just happy to be back to light duty, is all. It feels good to be back to work."

"Um, hum. Now tell me the real reason." She pulled her arm, making her wince.

"Fuck."

"Don't be a baby. You want to go back to patrol, right?"

"Yes."

"Then you need to deal with the pain. Plus… I don't think it's going to take four weeks. I think if we keep working like this, you'll be cleared in two."

"Seriously? Keep abusing me then." London laughed, giddy at the prospect of going back to full duty in less time.

"Well—it all depends."

"On what? I'll do whatever you want."

"Good—then answer my question?" Felicity arched an eyebrow and tapped her foot.

"You're the devil, woman." London shook her head as she followed his exercise routine. All the while, telling him about Davey. "So," she blew out a breath as she pushed the weight bar above her head, "I don't know what to do or think."

"You need to jump his bones," Felicity said matter of fact.

"Felicity." London pinked at her words.

"What? You're an attractive woman, London. And if I batted for the same team, I'd be pressing you against that bench right now. But I'm a professional—and straight." She smiled, making London even redder.

"What… I, um," London stuttered for words.

"Fuck… I'm kidding. You're not my type, seeing as you have a vagina. But it's fun too fuck with you."

"Well, geez, thanks."

"That's not what I mean," Felicity laughed. "You're an incredibly beautiful woman. But I'd rather bend your boyfriend over." She winked, drawing a smile out of London. Felicity has seen Davey around and mentioned on more than one occasion how hot he was.

London couldn't contain her laugh. "Christ… you're a real mess."

"It's true. I might be all brute in here—but it's my job to get you healed. But just because I'm with someone doesn't mean I'm blind. And if I had someone who cared about me the way he cares about you, I'd be over the moon. Not all women are as lucky as you—sometimes we get the frogs while others get the prince. You know what I mean? So, tell me. What's stopping you?"

"Fear, I guess."

"Fear of what?" She seemed confused, then her eyes lit up. "Oh… I see. You're in love with him."

"What? No. I'm not." London didn't believe her own words. Was she in love with him? They'd only had sex once, but Davey had been there for her during her recovery. Making sure she was safe and cared for—and never asked for more.

"You're realizing I'm right, aren't you?"

"What if he can't handle my job? I won't stop being a police officer. Not for anyone." London closed her eyes and pushed the feeling of unease down.

"I seriously doubt he cares about your job. If he did, he wouldn't have been at the hospital with you. He wouldn't have put his life on hold to nurse you back to health. London," Felicity patted her back. "In the short time I've come to know you, I've realized something."

London looked at her new friend. "What have you realized?"

"You might be fearless on the job, but you're terrified of love."

London didn't respond. Instead, she shrugged and hurried to the shower. Dressing quickly, she bid Felicity farewell and headed to work.

Were Frank and Felicity, right?

Was she fearless in all things but love?

London pushed those thoughts away and took her place at the desk. She needed to get her head on straight—especially before dinner tonight.

25

London paced her kitchen. She was a bundle of nerves waiting for Davey to arrive and didn't know why. It wasn't like this was the first time in her house. She'd texted him when she got home, telling him to give her thirty minutes before heading over. Now, thirty minutes later, she was beginning to stress. The knock at the door nearly made her jump out of her skin. She smoothed the material of her dress down and opened the door.

"Davey." She moved to the side, ushering him inside. "Thanks for coming over." London smiled at him, watching as she walked towards the kitchen counter. He set down a bottle of wine and moved to grab two glasses from the cabinet. "Long day?" She raised an eyebrow in question.

"No…" he poured the liquid into the glasses and handed her one as he sipped his. He set his empty glass down and took hers from her hand. "I see you are out of your sling."

London moved her arm. "Yeah—Felicity says I'm healing faster than he expected. She says I'll likely be cleared to full duty in two weeks."

Davey reached out and grabbed her hand, lacing his fingers with hers. "Good, that will make this much easier."

He tugged her against his chest, slipping his free hand behind her neck and twining his fingers into her hair. He angled her face towards him and slanted his lips over hers. It was soft at first, but as London pressed her body into his, his tongue pried its way into her mouth.

She moaned against his mouth, savoring everything about his demanding kiss. Her hips arched into his, rubbing against his erection. Davey spun her around, his hand slipping from hers and moving down her back. Gripping her ass, he hoisted London onto the counter. He tugged her to the edge and pressed the evidence of his desire into her center. London threaded her hands into his hair, surprised there was no pain when she lifted her arm.

Davey slipped his hands beneath her dress, his rough palms caressing her bare skin. London wasn't wearing a bra because the dress didn't allow for it. Davey groaned when he felt her bare skin. His lips broke from hers and made a trail of fire as he kissed down her jaw, nipping her earlobe, and sucking on her neck.

"Davey." London breathed out, pulling his face to hers again. He kissed her as his hands slipped her dress over her head. London sucked in a breath, nervous about what he would think about seeing her scars.

"Beautiful," Davey pressed a kiss to her shoulder, then pelting her sensitive skin with kisses as he trailed her scars, still red and new. Sliding her legs closer to the edge, he trailed his lips down her chest, sucking each nipple before descending. Davey peppered her abdomen with his lips, swirling his tongue around her belly button. London lifted as he urged her panties off and tossed them to the floor. Completely naked, London sat before him.

"God, you're incredible." Davey leaned in and pressed a kiss to her mouth as he slipped a finger between her folds. London arched into him, moaning. "Do you know what you do to me, London?"

His finger worked inside of her, curling and teasing her g-spot. London felt the tension coiling in her gut, building until she couldn't contain the scream. Davey pushed her back until her body was flush against the cold marble counter. He pressed her legs apart, burying his face between her thighs. He drew his tongue in circles around her sensitive nub, sucking and biting it all while his fingers dancing inside her.

"Davey…" She moaned his name. Writhing beneath his sensual assault on her throbbing center. Just when she didn't think she could take anymore, Davey curled his fingers inside her and pressed against her womb. His teeth grazed her clit, creating the ultimate sensation as her orgasm burst from her core. He lapped up her juices as London screamed in ecstasy.

"*Oh. My. God.*" London threw her arm over her face, sated but embarrassed. She was completely naked on her counter, while Davey stood completely dressed.

"Don't cover yourself. We're not done yet." He pulled her into his arms.

London instinctively wrapped her legs around him as he carried her towards the bedroom. She wiggled her center on his erection, still hidden beneath his jeans. Davey tossed her onto the bed, stripping his shirt as he approached her like a predator seeking prey.

"Those as well." London pointed towards his pants.

Davey shucked them off, losing his boxers and standing before her completely nude. His cock bounced against his belly button, reminding London of the first time they'd been together. It was long and thick, begging for her touch.

She tried to sit up, but Davey pressed his palm to her chest. "No. I need to be inside you. Please. I've waited too long."

His words were filled with tenderness and pain. But good pain. The kind that told her he'd been holding out. He kneed her legs apart and settled between her. Her pussy was hot and wet, begging for him to bury his dick inside her. Grabbing the condom from his discarded jeans, he sheathed himself in record time. London arched her back, pressing her folds against the head of his cock.

"Please, Davey."

That was all it took. He thrust his hips, burying himself deep inside her walls. Her pussy clamped on to his member, squeezing him tight. "Fuck, you're so tight, London."

She arched, begging him silently to move. Davey began thrusting his hips, sliding in and out of her channel. She felt so good wrapped around his cock. He closed his eyes, willing himself to go slow, but she felt so damn good. Her fingernails scratched at his back as her legs wrapped around his ass. She pushed him deeper, moaning as she clamped down, her orgasm washing over him.

Davey increased his speed, swirling his hips against her. He grabbed her legs, tossing one over his shoulder so he could press deeper. She let out a throaty moan, gripping his shoulders as her head arched back. She was close. So was he. Davey slipped his free hand beneath her ass, pressing into her harder.

His cock swelled as her cunt constricted around his shaft. Her orgasm took over, squeezing his cock with everything she had. Davey was sure his seed would burst through the condom as violent as his orgasm was. It was unlike anything he'd ever experienced.

Collapsing, Davey pressed a kiss to her forehead and rolled to his side. He pulled her against him. "Sorry—I couldn't go another day without being buried inside you."

London rested her hand on his chest, "What does this mean, Davey?" her words soft as she kissed his shoulder.

"Everything, London. It means everything." He let sleep take him. London pressed against his body felt like home.

26

London woke pressed against a hard body, her legs tangled with his. Davey. She smiled, remembering how he'd come into her house and essentially took what he wanted. Glancing at the clock, she realized it was well after ten. The sun had since set and they were covered in the moon's glow filtering through her blinds. Trying to untangle herself, Davey stirred beneath her.

"Hey." He pressed a kiss to her head.

"Hey, you. I need to pee. Be right back." London slipped from under his arm and rushed into the safety of her bathroom. Closing the door, she pressed her head against the cool wood. Her emotions were all over the place. Excitement, fear, and something else. Something she wasn't ready to give a name. A tap at the door startled her.

"London? You alright?"

Easing the door open, "Yeah. Sorry. Be out in a minute." Davey pushed his way inside.

"Don't shut me out, London."

"I'm not. Just need to pee. Preferably without you watching." She smiled, hiding the terror she felt looking at him. He pulled her chin up, placing a kiss on her lips.

"I'll go find something to eat. Don't be long."

London watched as he pulled his boxer briefs on, the tight fabric leaving little to the imagination. Once out of the room, London used the bathroom, splashed water on her face, and stepped into her bedroom. Glancing around, she caught sight of his shirt. It was adorned with the Station 19 logo. Smiling, she slipped it over her head. Grinning wider when she realized her arm no longer tingled when she did. Running her fingers through her hair, she hurried from her room. London was shocked to find Davey at her stove. His muscles flexed and tightened as he stirred the pan.

"I made stir fry. I hope that's ok." He turned, dropping the spatula when he saw what she was wearing. He turned the flame off and slowly slaked towards her. "You're wearing my shirt." He stepped close to her.

"I didn't think you'd mind."

"I don't. It looks good on you." Davey spun, grabbing the pan and dishing out food onto plates. "We should eat before I take you back to the bedroom and have my way with you."

London took a bite, her eyes closed as she moaned around the fork, "God, this is good." She opened her eyes to see Davey staring at her. His Adam's apple bobbed as he swallowed.

"Glad you like it." He shovelled food into his mouth.

"Davey," London swallowed. "What's going on between us? I mean, I invited you over for dinner—but wasn't expecting this." She waved her fork between them.

"You disappointed?" He smiled.

"No," she blushed, "but I'm confused."

"London," Davey moved to stand beside her, "I have waited for you to come around and realize I wanted more than friendship. The night you left my apartment, you left with a misunderstanding. Then you were shot. And when I saw you on the ground bleeding out—and your heart stopped..." He closed his eyes, gathering himself, "I am pretty sure so did mine. London, I have spent the last few years avoiding relationships out of fear. Fear of letting myself fall in love, only to lose my heart again. I can't risk another heartbreak. Or that's what I told myself... until you."

London sucked in a breath, "I... I... don't know what to say."

"Nothing. Say nothing. I'm not asking for an answer, London. I just couldn't hide my feelings from you anymore." Davey took the empty plate from her and tossed it into the sink. He tugged her hands into his, pulling her towards him, "Now... let's go to bed. Enough talking."

London followed him to the bedroom, confusion swirling through her gut. Davey confessed he wanted her, but did he confess love? London was too afraid to ask. Instead, she just followed him into the bedroom.

27

Their time together fell into a routine. Davey would meet her every morning to send her off with a kiss, and they spent most nights together, even though Davey usually left before morning. London was slowly letting her guard down, but fear of him running when she returned to work kept her from letting her walls down completely. The day had finally arrived. London was cleared for full duty. She stepped out of the shower and wiped the fog from the glass. Her reflection stared back at her, the smile barely reaching her eyes.

She was happy that she was going to be back in the car riding with Frank, but a part of her worried this was leading to the end of her and Davey. And that scared her. Pulling her hair into a ponytail, she pulled on her t-shirt and pants. Slipping the brand-new vest over her chest, she ran her fingers across the hard surface.

Just two months ago, this same material saved her life. After getting her shirt zipped, she buckled her gun belt and holstered her weapon. Even though London's dominant arm wasn't injured, last week, she spent re-qualifying at the department range. Higher-ups needed to be sure she was fit for duty. After getting the clearance, she had her start date to return to duty.

Stepping outside, she wasn't shocked to see the ambulance parked at the curb. Alex was propped against the bumper, watching as Davey carried flowers toward her.

"I wanted to wish you luck." He smiled at her.

Taking the flowers, she inhaled their floral scent. "Thank you."

Davey leaned in and kissed her. "You excited?" Davey smiled as he pulled away from her.

"Yes. Nervous. It's almost like my first day."

"You'll do great. I know Frank is excited to have you back."

"Yeah, all he did was complain about the newbie."

Davey opened her car door. "Well… I need to get back. I just needed to wish you luck and kiss you." He pressed his lips to hers again. "But you don't want to be late." He smacked her on the butt and helped her into the car. "Call me later."

Davey rushed off, leaving London once again speechless. Her gut churned with worry. Davey acted like he was okay with her returning, but she wasn't so sure.

London pulled into the station a bundle of nerves. Frank met her at the door. "You ready, kiddo? I know I'm glad to have that tree hugger out of my car."

"Be nice, Frank. He's a rookie."

"That wasn't the issue, London. He was all about chakras and shit. Told me mine was out of line, and eating hotdogs was poison to my soul. Poison. Do you *hear* me?" Frank grunted as he slid into the passenger seat.

"How about we grab some breakfast?" London threw the car into gear. "A big fat greasy one."

"Hell yeah. That's why I needed you back. You complete me." Frank smiled as they headed towards the local diner. London parked the patrol car and got out. It felt good to be back behind the wheel. They had barely finished their meal when a call came out.

"Well… guess we're back in business." London smirked as she flicked the lights on and headed towards the address dispatch gave. It was a fight call. Since it was barely eleven, London was hopeful alcohol wasn't involved, but it *was* at the local bar. Chances of that wish were slim. London saw the ambulance pull in at the same time as them. "Really?" London glanced at Frank.

"Dispatch said someone inside needed help. Calm down London."

"Fine, let's go."

28

LLONDON PUSHED OPEN THE DOOR TO FIND A MAN LYING IN THE middle of the floor. He'd been knocked out with what looked like the bar stool now in pieces beside him.

Frank barked at the bartender. "What happened?"

"These two idiots were fighting over her." He pointed towards a woman standing next to another girl. She was sobbing and had a busted lip. London approached her. "Ma'am, can you tell me what happened?"

"That jack ass grabbed my ass when my boyfriend went to the bathroom. I slapped him, and he started calling me names. Mike, my boyfriend, came out and got in his face. That behemoth of a man shoved him, causing him to elbow me in the face."

"Alright, let's get EMS to check your face." Just as London moved to escort her out, the drunk started screaming at Frank.

"FUCK YOU! She slapped me… this is her fault." He jerked from Frank's grasp and moved towards London and the girl.

Frank scrambled, trying to get his arms around the monster of a man's body.

"Stop." Frank yelled. London pushed the girl towards the door, causing her to tumble into Davey and Alex, who'd just come through.

"Shit." London glanced briefly at Davey as he cussed.

London reacted quickly. Throwing a punch into the man's throat just as he broke free from Frank's hold. He clutched his neck and dropped to his knees, gasping for air. London wasted no time slapping the cuff on his wrist and spinning his arm around. Digging her knee into his back, she forced him to the floor. He struggled beneath her, refusing to give his other arm to her. "Get off me, bitch." He bucked, trying to throw her off. London saw Davey move out of the corner of her eye. Ignoring him, she applied pressure just below his ear. The man stopped fighting her, crying out in pain.

"Give me your hand." Slowly, he reached back, allowing London to cuff his other hand. Slipping off his back, London stood and smiled at Frank. "Nothing like breaking me in on my first day back. Maybe the rookie was right… you need to lay off the hotdogs."

Frank laughed, "Bite me, London."

She glanced towards Davey, who was smiling at her. He almost seemed proud. "Nah… my bites are reserved for someone else." Davey turned pink before walking towards her.

"Gross, London. I don't want to hear about your kinks."

London cocked her head, her eyes filled with mischief. "Really, Frank. You telling me you're no longer worried about my vagina?"

Davey glared at Frank, who put his hands in the air in submission. "Don't take it the wrong way, man. I just told her she needed a man. But it looks like she's finally taken my advice." Frank dragged the man in cuffs out the door, leaving Davey and London alone with the remaining patrons.

"You did good, London." He leaned into whisper in her ear. "My dick got hard watching you take him down." He brushed past her, making sure the hard bulge in his pants pressed against her. He found Alex, who'd just finished patching up the girl's lip. Liam Carver, a sergeant on patrol, was talking with her as London came out the door.

London couldn't believe he'd said that to her. Seeing her rough up a drunk turned him on? None of the other men she had dated ever told her that her job was a turn on. Her panties got wet just thinking about it.

"Hey, Davey," She called out as she approached her car. He turned just as he was pulling himself into the rig.

"I get off at six. But I'd like to get off later." She slid into the car and slammed the door. Looking in her rear-view mirror, she watched as Davey slipped off the running board and landed on his ass.

"That was dirty, London. I didn't know you had it in you." Frank smirked.

London blushed as her phone beeped with a text message.

Davey: Meet me at the station at 9.

"I don't want to know." Frank laughed. "Let's get this idiot to jail."

"No, you probably don't want to know. But—" London inhaled. "You're right."

"Right about what?"

She put the car in gear. "I'm a runner. And I'm done running."

"Bout fucking time." Frank slapped the dashboard. "You need to put him out of his misery."

London couldn't wait for her shift to end. For the first time in her life, work wasn't consuming her mind.

Her sexy ass paramedic was.

29

London had never been so nervous in her life. Even her first day of the academy wasn't this nerve-wracking. She knew without a doubt that she'd fallen head over heels in love with Davey. She only hoped he genuinely supported her career because it wasn't him or her job. It had to be both or none. Parking her car in a visitor space, she climbed out and headed into the bay area. Uri, Jonesy, and Dawson were seated at a small card table.

Dawson smiled as he stood and pulled her into a hug. "Glad to see you up and about. Heard you were back to work and already kicked some ass."

"Alex has a big mouth." London laughed as she pulled from his embrace.

"Not Alex. Davey. He wouldn't shut up about it. He just kept saying how hot it was to see you kick a man's ass."

London blushed. "Well, I work hard to be in shape, so I can take care of myself."

"Well," He spun her around, "You definitely look good. Davey's in his room. You remember how to get up there?"

"I think so. It was good to see you guys."

"Oh, and London," Uri sipped his coke. "We gotta do a fuel run. Let Davey know we'll be back."

London felt like it was a pre-planned coincidence. "Where's Alex?" Glancing around, she noted the ambulance was missing.

"Cap went with her to the hospital. Something about a screw up with inventory. They're out of service for a bit."

"Oh… ok. See you guys around." London pushed through the door and climbed the steps. Her stomach was in knots by the time she got to Davey's door. Taking a deep breath, she knocked. "Davey?"

He pulled the door open. "Come in."

Stepping to the side and closing the door behind her. London had barely made it in the room before Davey had her hand and spun her back to the door.

"I missed you." He pressed his lips to hers. "Seeing you on that call," he pressed his lips to her neck, "was fucking hot. London, you're amazing at what you do." He licked her collarbone, his hands dropping to her ass as he lifted her feet off the ground. His hip ground into her center as he pushed her dress up. "Did you wear this for me?" He smiled, slipping his hands beneath the fabric.

"Yes." London moaned as his erection rubbed against her clit.

"Do you have any idea what you do to me? How much I want to bury myself inside you every minute of every day? That little stunt you pulled this afternoon left me in an uncomfortable position. It was quite difficult hiding my reaction from Alex."

London ran her hand down between them, squeezing his cock, nearly bursting beneath his uniform pants. His hips bucked, a moan escaping his lips. "I want you." His hot breath caressed her ear as he kissed the curve of her neck.

"I'm yours. Take me, Davey."

Davey spun them around and laid her on his bunk. The bed was small, but he didn't care. Davey needed to be inside her. Pulling his shirt over his head, he unbuckled his belt. And pushed them to his feet. Pulling London's panties to the side, he slipped a finger inside and groaned. "Your so wet."

"Only for you." She bucked her hips, hissing as he pressed his lips to her pink folds. She thrashed and moaned as he licked her slit, nibbling her tiny bundle of nerves. Her orgasm built, bursting like a damn, as she screamed out his name.

Davey licked his finger as he climbed her body and then pressed his mouth to hers. He positioned his painfully hard cock between her legs and pushed inside. London felt immediately full, her walls tightening to hold him inside. She moved, silently pleading for him to give her what she desired. Davey thrust slowly, easing in and out.

When London locked her feet behind his hips, Davey lost control and pounded her harder. He was like an addict trying to reach his all-time high. Their breaths were ragged as they raced towards the finish line. He knew the moment she was about to let go. Her walls started tensing, gripping his cock like its life depended on it. He flexed his hips, pressing deeper as her orgasm burst like fireworks on the fourth of July.

As she screamed his name, Davey let go, letting his orgasm wash over him. Panting, he pushed himself up. London was glowing, her cheeks flushed. Davey slipped free, discarding the condom. He grabbed a nearby towel and cleaned himself off, then cleaned her.

Tucking himself into his pants, "God damn you make me crazy." He laughed as he pulled her to a seated position and put her panties back in place.

"Is that a bad thing?"

Dave squeezed her. "No… not at all."

"You hungry?"

London looked at him longingly. "Famished."

He chuckled, knowing exactly what she meant. "Let's go grab some food before the others get back."

London let him pull her up and guide her out of the room. Their lovemaking was fast, but she loved every minute. London wondered why he hadn't said anything more, and part of her worried he didn't feel the same as she did. She pushed that aside as she followed him down the stairs and into the kitchen. Eventually, she would tell him how she was feeling.

30

THE REST OF THE GUYS, INCLUDING ALEX, MADE IT BACK TO THE station when Davey and London were eating in the dining hall. London watched as the guys filtered in and grabbed food.

Alex was the first to speak. "Looking mighty, radiant, London. Having a good night?" She smirked at her friend.

London couldn't hide the blush. "Shut up, Alex."

"Davey, you too."

Davey fisted a biscuit, pretending to aim it at her head. "Alex… don't make me throw this at you."

"Oh, calm down… I'm just fucking with you."

"I'm pretty sure Alex was the same shade of pink when Dr. Williams was around. That man is smitten with you, girl."

"Dr. Williams, huh?"

Alex looked down at her food. "Um… yeah, I guess."

"I thought he was into you that day in my room."

"We're just friends. Besides, I want to know what's going on with you two? Didn't you both say you didn't do relationships or date?"

London froze. She and Davey hadn't talked about what they were doing, so she didn't know what to say.

Davey answered for them, "Yeah… we did. And I don't date."

London's heart bottomed out. Exactly what she was afraid of was playing out in front of his entire shift. "Um… I got to go." London glanced at Alex. "Call you later." She went to rush around Davey, but he grabbed her arm.

"I don't date because I have everything I need right here." He tugged London into his arms. "I love you, London. I don't need anyone else because you're it for me." His eyes watched her for a reaction.

London didn't notice the room had become completely empty except for them. She froze. "Davey," she was interrupted by the alarm. EMS was being called to the scene of a fire.

"Shit… will you wait here for me?"

London nodded, following him towards the truck. She watched as he grabbed his gear and headed towards the truck. "Davey!" She called out. He turned towards her as he was easing into the driver's seat.

"Yeah?"

"I love you, too." She smiled as his face fill with utter shock. "I'll see you when you get back."

London watched as they pulled from the station. She'd be here waiting for him when he returned. London had waited an eternity for a man like him. Hanging out while he was on a call was nothing to her.

When they finally got back to the station, it was nearly the end of the shift. The fire had wiped out two houses, but no casualties resulted. Davey was covered in soot and wanted to crawl into his bed, even if it was just a few hours of sleep before he got off. He'd texted London from the scene, telling her it would be a while before he'd be back. She'd told him to be safe, and she'd see him later.

He didn't expect her to be there when he got back, so when Davey walked into his room and found her sound asleep on his bunk, he couldn't stop the smile from taking over his face. Davey stripped his ruined uniform and grabbed a quick shower. He slipped into bed beside her after donning a pair of boxers.

The small twin bed put them in close quarters, but Davey didn't mind. He pulled her back to his chest and cradled her body to his. London stirred briefly as Davey wrapped his arm around her. Davey felt more at home with her in his arms than he had in a long time. For the first time since losing Carley, he felt at peace. And it had everything to do with the woman in his arms. Davey didn't plan on waiting a minute longer. Tomorrow, he would tell her what he wanted. He prayed she wouldn't run. Closing his eyes, it didn't take long for the exhaustion to take over and him to fall asleep with her in his arms.

31

LONDON WOKE WRAPPED IN DAVEY'S ARMS. GLANCING AT THE clock, she cursed. She had to be at work in an hour. "Davey," she pried his arms from her waist, "I have to go."

"What time is it?"

"Five. I go on shift at Six. I need to get home and change."

"Damn. My shift's almost over, anyway." He pushed himself up, nearly knocking her off the bed. "Shit… you alright?"

"Yeah…" London stood, stretching her arms above her head. Her dress rose, revealing the globes of her ass to Davey.

He swatted her butt. "You sure you can't call in sick?"

London spun, "Davey. It's my second day back."

"I was kidding. Seriously," He stood, pulling her towards him and kissing her. "I know this is important. Can I see you tonight?"

"Yes. Now… I have to leave." London pulled the door open. "Am I going to get you in trouble? Should I sneak out?"

"Nah… Captain knew you were here. It's alright. A lot of the wives come and sleep here."

"Yeah… I'm not your wife, though."

Davey smiled, "It's fine, London. I'll see you tonight." He kissed her again before pushing her out the door. "Now go… before I make you late."

"Davey," London glanced over her shoulder, "I love you. See you tonight." She bolted down the steps, taking them two at a time. Davey got down the steps just in time to see her car pulling out.

"You got it bad, brother." Uri clapped him on the back.

"I love her." Davey smiled at his friend.

Two hours later, he grabbed his bag and clocked out. Rushing to his truck, he pulled out his phone.

Davey: I love you, London. Have a good day. Be safe. See you tonight.

London: love you too. ;-)

Davey tapped his phone. He wanted to make tonight special because he had something important to ask her. Scrolling through his phone, Davey called his sister and then Carrie. He would need their help for this to be just right. Smiling after getting Carrie to agree and help him, he slipped his phone into his pocket and started his truck. He needed to run into town and grab a few things to make this plan work.

London was bone tired when her shift finally ended. A multitude of domestics and two car accidents left her begging for a hot bath and a glass of wine. She was relieved to have the next three days off. Pulling into her driveway, she was surprised to see Davey's truck on the curb. Hopping out of her car, she realized he wasn't sitting inside the cab. She glanced toward her house, noticing that the lights were on in the kitchen. For a moment she wondered how he got in, but remembered she'd never asked for her key back when he stayed during her recovery.

Slowly climbing the steps, she eased the door open. "Davey?" She called out. Soft music filled the room. London noticed candles lining the shelves, and flower petals were splayed all over the floor. London unclasped her gun belt, laying it on the entry table. She tossed her keys down and followed the floral path. London stopped when she got to the kitchen, her breath caught in her chest when she found Davey kneeling.

"London," He smiled at her, "When I lost my fiancé, Carley, I swore I'd never risk my heart to another. But then I met this fiery, stubborn, kick-ass woman. She broke through my façade and took down the walls guarding my heart. Her spirit was unlike anything I've ever felt or seen. London," He took her hand in his, "you are so damn strong. You don't take crap from anyone, and I'm pretty sure you could kick my ass." Davey laughed. "I don't want to change you. I love you just the way you are, and I would love nothing more than to make you my wife. What do you say, Officer Brett? Will you marry me?" Davey held out the most stunning band. Two rows of diamonds lined a row of blue stones in the middle. London couldn't stop the tears from spilling down her face.

"Davey," she pressed her hand to his cheek, "I don't know what to say." She laughed.

"Say yes, London. Let me love you for the rest of our lives. Let me be the man you stand beside. The one you come home to, the one you raise a family with." Davey held his breath, praying her answer was going to be yes.

32

"Yes… A million times, yes."

Davey released the air from his lungs as he slipped the ring on to her finger. He stood and pulled her into a hug. Davey lifted her body as she wrapped her legs around his waist. Moving towards the bedroom, Davey couldn't stop kissing her lips as he headed down the hallway.

Pushing the door open, Davey put her on her feet. He pulled her shirt free of her pants and unzipped it, and tossed it to the floor. He released the Velcro of her vest and slipped it over her head. It made an awful thud as it hit the floor. "God damn, you have on too many layers." Davey ripped her t-shirt straight down the middle, causing London to inhale suddenly. She giggled when he caught sight of her sports bra and raised an eyebrow.

"What? It's comfortable at work." London giggled but gasped when he ripped it off as well. Davey tossed the scrap to the floor and pressed his mouth to her very erect nipple. Her pink flesh was warm as he drew it between his lips. London leaned back, arching her chest into his touch. Davey slid his hands down her body, releasing the button to her pants and shoving them to the floor. Pulling his mouth from her nipple, his lips popped from the suction. Davey pushed her back to the bed and reached down to remove her boots. He threw them over his shoulder, yanking her pants, socks, and panties off in one fluid motion. London laid utterly bare to him. Standing back up, Davey shucked his clothes and stood before her with his cock fisted in his hands. "I'm going to make love to you, London. Do you want that?"

"Yes… Davey, please," She begged.

Davey pressed her legs open, making room for his shoulders as he buried his face between her folds. He wasted no time tasting and sucking her flesh. London wrapped her legs around his head, bucking and thrusting as his tongue made contact with her clit. Her whole body was on fire. Clawing at him, she let her orgasm spill into his mouth. Davey lapped up the sweet nectar, sucking the juice from her soft lips. Slowly, he made his way up her body, kissing and biting the tender skin.

"London," Davey whispered, "I want to feel your pussy on my cock without something between us." London leaned up on her elbows, knowing what he was asking. They'd never had sex without a condom before.

"I'm on the pill."

It was all Davey needed. He pressed his dick into her folds, filling her womb up to the hilt. Once he was fully seated, he paused, relishing in the feel of her cunt sucking on his cock. London fidgeted below him, wiggling her hips, silently urging him to move. Davey drew back, the tip of his penis easing out slightly before he plunged back inside.

London moaned, crying out with each thrust. Gripping her leg, he pushed deeper, seeking the orgasm from her he knew was close. London let out a guttural scream as her walls spasmed around his member. Davey grabbed her hips, flipping them over, so she was on top. Pressing her hips, he rocked her, her nub rubbing against his pelvic bone. The angle was perfect, as he pushed her towards another release. London pressed her palms into his chest, taking control of her movements.

She leaned down, pressing her hips into him, and lifted her ass. Her cunt was slick and glided across his cock perfectly.

"That's it, baby. Take what you want from me." Davey grunted out as she bounced on his dick.

She was lost with reckless abandon, as she was trapped in a sensual dance with his cock. Her pussy tightened, her body going taunt as her orgasm burst free. She screamed out into the room, bouncing through her release. Davey lifted her body, flipping her over onto her stomach. He slammed his dick into her channel, pulling her ass up and pressing her chest to the bed. The angle allowed him to reach depths he didn't know were possible.

Reaching around, he pinched her nub, "Give me one more, London."

"I can't..." She whimpered, her body glistening with a sheen of sweat.

He pounded into her. "You can."

The sound of their bodies slapping filled the room. His finger caressed the sensitive bud, forcing her to come again.

"Oh God… Davey, I'm coming again," She squealed.

Once again, her pussy clamped down on him. Her walls suffocating his cock inside as she milked him for everything he had. His seed spilled from him, his cock pulsing inside her. Even as he collapsed, still buried inside her, his cock continued to twitch while his come kept spurting.

"Fuck," he panted. Rolling to his side. "London, you're going to kill me." He laughed.

"But what a way to die." She smiled, rolling into his chest.

"God, I love you." Davey pressed a kiss to her forehead, rubbing his hand down her naked back.

"And I love you. Holy shit. We're getting married." She sat up. "I need to call my dad and Carrie."

"They know." He pulled her back down, tucking her into his side. "I asked your dad's permission, and Carrie helped me set up the house. I promised them we'd meet for breakfast tomorrow."

"You asked my dad?"

"Yep. And my parents will be there tomorrow as well. Oh," he took a breath. "And my sister and brother. So we should get some sleep."

"Sleep?" London leaned up on her elbows and smirked.

"Yes… we have to meet at eight."

London smiled, easing herself to lie on his chest, "I'm not tired…" She cocked an eyebrow and started kissing down his chest.

"London, we really…" his words died on his lips when she took him into her mouth. Davey hissed, "Fuck."

"Still tired?" London peeked up from beneath the covers.

"Um, what?" Davey opened an eye to glance at her. "No… not at all."

London smiled before swallowing his cock. She didn't care if they walked into breakfast, looking like the Walking Dead. Right now, all she wanted was to taste him and give him pleasure.

After two more rounds of lovemaking, Davey and London collapsed in each other's arms.

"Thank you for letting me love you, London."

"No, Davey. Thank you for showing me what unconditional love is… I love you."

33

This was it. Today was the day London would become Mrs. Davey Patrick. Carrie was running around, trying to ensure everything was perfect. Her dad had already shed tears, saying how he wished her mother could see her. London tried to stay calm. The last thing she wanted was to ruin her make-up. Alex and Harley were her only two bridesmaids, Carrie, her maid of honor. She and Davey had a small wedding, inviting only friends and immediate family.

Davey asked his brother Steven to stand as his best man, leaving Uri and Jonesy to stand in as groom's men.

And unknown to London, her sister Carrie and Steven had been seeing each other. Carrie finally spilled the beans after Davey tried to set her up with Uri. Funny enough, Uri and Harley seemed to be getting pretty cosy.

Frank and his wife Kathy sat along with Liam Carver and Finn Judson, fellow officers who were also friends with the guys from station six. Frank had finally retired at the end of the year, leaving London with the tree hugger for a partner. At first, Davey was jealous, but once he learned Adam, her new partner, was seeing a guy name Max, he calmed down. Also among the guests was her Physical therapist, Felicity. At first Felicity declined her invite, saying her boyfriend had to work—but at the last minute came alone.

It'd been a year since London was shot. Since then, her priorities had shifted some. While the job was vital to her… her soon to be husband was more important—and that was shocking even to her.

Davey had asked her where she saw herself going in the department, and until recently, she thought she'd stay on patrol forever. She'd even been offered a promotion to patrol sergeant, but circumstances change. Davey kept asking her why she hadn't accepted, but the surprise she had for her soon to be husband would change the course of their life forever, making him understand her hesitation.

Carrie interrupted her thoughts. "You ready?"

"Yes—where's dad?"

"Waiting outside. I'll meet you at the altar. I'm so happy for you, London. Mom would be proud."

"I wish she was here."

"She is…" Carrie squeezed her hand and escorted her to their father, waiting just outside the door.

"You ready, squirt?"

London teared up. "Dad…"

"I'm so proud of you, London. And Davey is a good man. I'll be proud to call him my son."

London squeezed his arm as they walked towards her forever.

Davey couldn't take his eyes off his new bride as they had their first dance as husband and wife. He never thought he'd have this chance again. Losing Carley practically broke him. Then, nearly losing London sent him over the edge. He knew, at that moment, she was meant to be his forever. Holding her against his chest, swaying to the music, he felt like nothing could get better. Having her in his arms was near perfection.

"Have you decided whether you're going to take the promotion? You know I support whatever you decide."

"I know. But I'm not sure if staying on patrol is what I want right now."

Davey spun her out as he tugged her back towards him. "What? You love patrol, London."

"I do… but I love our family more." She buried her head in the crook of his neck, waiting for his reaction.

"Our family will support you, just like I will."

"It's not that, Davey," she smiled against him. "Patrol is dangerous. I can't put our baby at risk like that."

Davey kept swaying. "I know it's dangerous. But—" He stopped moving, his eyes blazing with understanding. "Baby?" He pushed her back, looking her up and down. "You're—" He shook his head as if he was trying to ensure it wasn't a dream.

"Pregnant." She answered. "Six weeks. I found out a few days ago. I know we weren't planning on this, but…" her voice trailed off.

Davey lifted her into his arms and spun them around. "A baby… I'm going to be a dad!" He hollered, not caring who heard him. "Did you hear that, everyone? I'm going to be a dad!" He put London down on her feet and kissed her like a man deeply in love. Davey didn't give two shits their entire family was watching. He was beyond happy. Everyone gathered around them, congratulating them. London's dad cried, so did Davey's mom.

When they finally left the reception, London's face hurt from all the smiling. "Are you really happy?" Turning towards Davey as she waited for his reply.

"Happy?" Davey placed his hand on her still flat stomach. "There are no words to describe what I am feeling right now, Mrs. Patrick. You have given me more than I deserve. I plan on showing you just how happy I am for the rest of our lives." Davey helped London from the truck and tossed the valet his keys. "Now, I want to take my wife up to our hotel room and remind her just how we made a life together."

Davey scooped her into his arms and carried her to the elevator. Strangers turned and gawked, seeing him in his tuxedo and her still in her wedding gown. Davey didn't put her down until they were inside their hotel room.

"I love you, Mrs. Patrick."

"I love you, Mr. Patrick." She pressed her lips to his. "Now, help me out of this dress. I remember you promising to show me how we made this tiny life growing inside me."

Davey undressed her, then removed his clothes, and laid her down on the bed. "Gladly. Wife."

London pressed her hand to his cheek, "Make love to me as my husband."

Davey wasted no more time on words. They spent the night making love. Davey knew that forever would not be long enough to show London his love, but he wouldn't waste a single minute of their time. Davey wrapped his arms around his new bride. He closed his eyes and gave in to the sleep, calling him.

London smiled as her husband held her close. She was grateful she didn't let her fear keep her from experiencing the love Davey had given her.

She burrowed deeper into his hold, his breaths evened out, signaling he'd fallen asleep. London couldn't stop smiling. They'd broken down each other's walls and revived the love they'd thought they'd lost.

Davey showed her the meaning of a partner.

He didn't stand in front of her or behind her.

No... He stood *beside* her.

EPILOGUE

Liam Carver stood back and watched as two of his friends danced together as husband and wife. He couldn't help being jealous… he thought that would be him—but life can really kick you in the balls sometimes.

"They make the perfect couple, don't they?" Finn slid beside him.

Liam glanced over at his friend and co-worker. "Maybe you'll be next."

"Nah." He shook his head. "Tried that once before, and it didn't work out, remember?"

Liam nodded. He'd heard the story plenty. Finn's wife had an affair and destroyed their marriage. It had turned him off from anything serious since. "What about you?"

Liam shrugged. "Not for me either."

Finn nodded in understanding. "Guess we'll just be bachelors together."

Liam laughed at Finn, his gut silently twisting at that reality. He could have any woman he wanted—he knew that. And it wasn't that he was full of himself, but women flocked to the uniform. Some were just badge bunnies, but others wanted something serious. Liam didn't want that with anyone. His heart had been ripped out by his high school sweetheart a decade ago. She'd gone off looking for greener pastures—while he stayed here.

As if some electric force had zapped him, Liam turned his head toward a group of London's friends. He knew several of the women huddled together, but one in particular had his breath catching in his chest.

"You alright?" Finn slapped him on the back. "You look like you've seen a ghost."

Liam pushed off the wall he was leaning against. "I have to go. Tell everyone I'll see them around."

"Whoa… what the hell happened?" Finn's eyes scanned the area, trying to see what spooked Liam.

Liam's eyes zeroed in on the woman standing beside Carrie, the bride's sister. Finn followed his line of sight, then looked back at Liam.

"You know her or something."

Liam took a deep breath, his eyes finally turning toward his friend. "Or something. I'll see you later, Finn."

Finn watched with a slack jaw as Liam turned and stormed from the wedding reception. Liam felt bad rushing out without telling London and Davey congratulations, but Finn had been right—he'd seen a ghost, and it spooked him.

Glancing in his rear-view mirror, Liam shook his head. Never in his wildest dreams did he ever think the two of them would cross paths again.

But that was a reality, not a dream.

And as sure as his next breath, he had every intention of finding out why she was back—and, more important than that.

Liam needed to know why his heart felt like it was beating out of his chest just from the sight of *her*.

Can two hearts find their way back to where they belong?
Find out in Signal 99: Freeing Felicity

ALSO BY LC TAYLOR

Simply scan the QR code to find your next great read.

Can't scan?

No worries… simply visit

www.behindthebadgepress.com

ABOUT THE AUTHOR

"Grab me a shot of whiskey. These books are about tattooed men and guns!"

What can I say? I'm a down home southern girl who bleeds red, white, and blue, so welcome to My world. I'm an International and USA Today best-selling author, who's an unapologetic down-home southern gal, with a bit of a dirty mouth.

But… I've never met a brooding hero I didn't love. I write my men cut, tattooed and tender, for their down, but-not-out ladies, who just need a little love from the right man.

When I'm not writing my Crossroads Heroes series, creating swoon-worthy love connections, or indulging my darker desires as my alter ego Dori P, I'm curled up with a glass of peach crown and my very own sexy tattooed cop on the couch watching reruns of Chicago Fire..

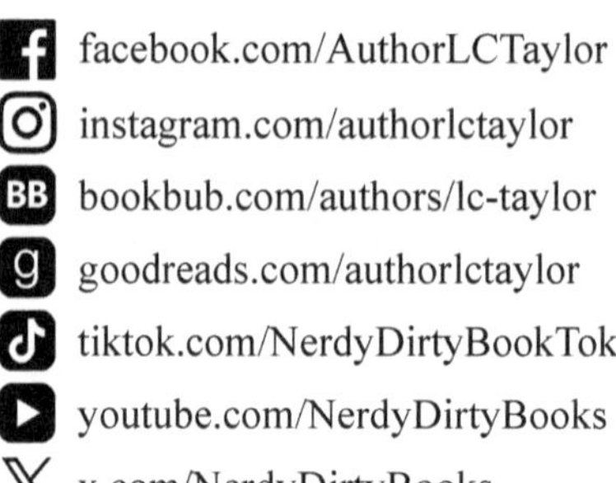

facebook.com/AuthorLCTaylor
instagram.com/authorlctaylor
bookbub.com/authors/lc-taylor
goodreads.com/authorlctaylor
tiktok.com/NerdyDirtyBookTok
youtube.com/NerdyDirtyBooks
x.com/NerdyDirtyBooks